Hi, I'm JIMMY!

Like me, you probably noticed the world is run by adults.
But ask yourself: Who would do the best job
of making books that *kids* will love?
Yeah. **Kids!**

So that's how the idea of JIMMY books came to life.
We want every JIMMY book to be so good
that when you're finished, you'll say,
"PLEASE GIVE ME ANOTHER BOOK!"

Give this one a try and see if you agree.
(If not, you're probably an adult!)

JIMMY Patterson Books for Young Readers

JAMES PATTERSON PRESENTS
Sci-Fi Junior High by John Martin and Scott Seegert
Sci-Fi Junior High: Crash Landing by John Martin and Scott Seegert
How to Be a Supervillain by Michael Fry
How to Be a Supervillain: Born to Be Good by Michael Fry
How to Be a Supervillain: Bad Guys Finish First by Michael Fry
The Unflushables by Ron Bates
Ernestine, Catastrophe Queen by Merrill Wyatt
Scouts by Shannon Greenland
No More Monsters Under Your Bed! by Jordan Chouteau
There Was an Old Woman Who Lived in a Book by Jomike Tejido
The Ugly Doodles by Valeria Wicker
Sweet Child O' Mine by Guns N' Roses
The Family that Cooks Together by Anna and Madeline Zakarian, daughters of Geoffrey Zakarian
The Day the Kids Took Over by Sam Apple

THE MIDDLE SCHOOL SERIES BY JAMES PATTERSON
Middle School, The Worst Years of My Life
Middle School: Get Me Out of Here!
Middle School: Big Fat Liar
Middle School: How I Survived Bullies, Broccoli, and Snake Hill
Middle School: Ultimate Showdown
Middle School: Save Rafe!
Middle School: Just My Rotten Luck
Middle School: Dog's Best Friend
Middle School: Escape to Australia
Middle School: From Hero to Zero
Middle School: Born to Rock
Middle School: Master of Disaster
Middle School: Field Trip Fiasco

THE I FUNNY SERIES BY JAMES PATTERSON
I Funny
I Even Funnier
I Totally Funniest
I Funny TV
I Funny: School of Laughs
The Nerdiest, Wimpiest, Dorkiest I Funny Ever

DOG DIARIES
DOUBLE DOG DARE

JAMES PATTERSON
WITH STEVEN BUTLER
ILLUSTRATED BY RICHARD WATSON

JIMMY Patterson Books
Little, Brown and Company
New York   Boston   London

Copyright © 2020 by James Patterson

Hachette Book Group supports the right to free expression and the value of copyright. The purpose of copyright is to encourage writers and artists to produce the creative works that enrich our culture.

The scanning, uploading, and distribution of this book without permission is a theft of the author's intellectual property. If you would like permission to use material from the book (other than for review purposes), please contact permissions@hbgusa.com. Thank you for your support of the author's rights.

JIMMY Patterson Books / Little, Brown and Company
Hachette Book Group
1290 Avenue of the Americas, New York, NY 10104
JamesPatterson.com
facebook.com/JimmyPattersonBooks
twitter.com/Jimmy_Books

Dog Diaries originally published in Great Britain by
Penguin Random House UK, May 2018
Dog Diaries: Happy Howlidays first published in Great Britain by
Penguin Random House UK, November 2018
First North American edition of *Dog Diaries* published in hardcover by
Little, Brown & Company, December 2018.
First North American edition of *Dog Diaries: Happy Howlidays* published in
hardcover by Little, Brown & Company, October 2019

JIMMY Patterson Books is an imprint of Little, Brown and Company, a division of Hachette Book Group, Inc. The Little, Brown name and logo are trademarks of Hachette Book Group, Inc. The JIMMY Patterson Books® name and logo are trademarks of JBP Business, LLC.

The publisher is not responsible for websites (or their content) that are not owned by the publisher.

The Hachette Speakers Bureau provides a wide range of authors for speaking events. To find out more, go to hachettespeakersbureau.com or call (866) 376-6591.

ISBN 978-0-316-49909-5

Cataloging-in-Publication data is available at the Library of Congress

LSC-H

Printing 2, 2021

THE FIRST BOOK FOR KIDS WRITTEN BY A DOG!

DOG DIARIES

A MIDDLE SCHOOL STORY

CREATOR OF *MAX EINSTEIN*

JAMES PATTERSON

WITH STEVEN BUTLER

DOG DIARIES

A MIDDLE SCHOOL STORY

JAMES PATTERSON

WITH STEVEN BUTLER
ILLUSTRATED BY RICHARD WATSON

OOOOOOH! You opened it! You actually opened my book!

I've been waiting for ages, and now a human-youngling is finally reading the beginning of my story.

This sure is a waggy-tail-icious moment! I don't think I've been this excited since... since... since I spotted a raccoon out by the trash cans and chased it up a fence!

That was a good day…IT WAS TERRIFIC…
one of the greatest, but this is even greater!

I love humans, and I bet you're a really tre-
mendous one.

Oh boy, oh boy, oh boy!

Okay, I need to calm down a little if we're
going to get this story told.

Hmmm…what to do first?

Oh yeah! Here's a gift just for you. It'd be
rude of me not to share my best-best-BEST
treasure.

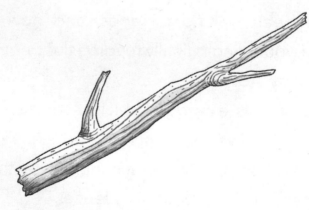

MY FAVORITE STICK!

It's yours, I insist. One end is a little chewed, but the rest of it is excellent. Don't crunch it all at once.

There—now you're my really real person-pal and we can start the story properly.

Sit!

Sit!

Down!

Ha ha...I've always wanted to say that to a human.

Okay. If you're comfortable, I'll begin...

I remember it like it was yesterday.

The happiest moment of a mutt's life, when you see your pet human for the first time, and you know instantly that you're going to be BEST FRIENDS forever.

That's how it was when I met mine, and OH BOY do I have a great pet. But I'm getting ahead of myself. You don't even know who I am.

I should probably start this story the way you humans like to, with an introduction. Us pooches don't normally bother with things like that. We usually prefer to take a polite sniff of each other's butts and—HEY PRESTO!—we've got all the information we need. But for you, my non-furry reader, I'll make an exception.

My name is Junior—hello! Or should I say, HERROOOOOOOOOOOOOOOOOOW?

If you hadn't guessed already, I'm a dog. Yep...shiny-nosed...licky-tongued...floppy-eared...bow-wow-woof-woof...and you're holding my daily doggy diary in your five fingery digits.

Consider yourself extremely lucky, my person-pal. In this book, you'll find the story of my life so far with my brand-new family, and it's a HUMDINGER!

Now, I know what you're thinking. You're sitting there, wrinkling up your forehead as we speak, saying "A dog's diary?" to yourself and picturing my furry little paws typing away at a computer or scribbling in a notebook. Don't be so people-brained... Ha!

You may also be wondering why on earth I would be keeping a journal. That's what princesses locked in towers, or grandmoos and grand-paws get up to, right?

WRONG!

In case you didn't know, all canines keep diaries. IT'S TRUE! We always have, ever since the DAWN OF DOG...all the way back to the time of the cavepeople and their saber-toothed terriers...

Just not in the same way that humans might.

Why do you think we all stop to sniff every corner and streetlight and fire hydrant on our morning walk?

Never thought about it, huh?

Well, I'll tell you.

We're snooping on the local gossip,

checking who's been around, and generally keeping up to date with what's happening in the neighborhood. To us, having a good snuffle is like reading the news.

You see, dogs keep smell diaries. Every pee and poop tells a tale, dontchaknow? But let's not panic just yet. I'm not about to ask you to stop and sniff my...ummm...you-know-what.

Nope, with the help of some booky brain-iac humans, my story has been written down. Incredible, huh? They can do ANYTHING nowadays. And you can safely enjoy every word without having to worry about all the whiffs and stinks. IT'S EXCELLENT! EVERY-BODY WINS!

So, where was I?

Oh, yeah, my pet human. I guess the day I came to live with him and his family is the best place to begin my diary. It's my happiest day of them all, so far.

Only last year, my life was a seriously different bowl of kibble.

Like so many of my furry friends, I was serving life in the slammer...the clink...pooch prison!

You guessed it. My luck had run out and I found myself locked away in the scariest place in the whole world. Scratch that—THE WHOLE UNIVERSE!

HILLS VILLAGE DOG SHELTER!

There are no ear scratches or belly rubs or nose boops in that place, let me tell you. No siree! The humans who work there shuffle past, ignoring you, and don't even want to play ball! I KNOW! IT'S HORRIFIC!

That place is one great big boredom-fest. It's enough to turn even the bounciest pup into a small microbe of misery in no time.

BUT... I'm not there now, ha ha!

Yipp-yipp-yippee, I can't wait to tell you this part.

All righty. Do you have spare snacks to keep us both happy as we scamper through the next few pages together?

You do?

EXCELLENT!

The First Day:
A Lot of Tuesdays Ago...

I was sitting in the backyard of a house with the old lady called Grandmoo who smells like ointment and bug spray, the Mom-Lady, and the little one with a voice like a dog whistle staring down at me.

Mom-Lady had collected me from the shelter earlier that day, and it was all SO EXCITING! She bought me a new green collar with a jingly tag on it, and I got to ride up

~~GRANDMA~~
Grandmoo

~~MOM~~
Mom-Lady

~~GEORGIA~~
Jawjaw

front in one of those moving people-boxes on wheels. I had to concentrate really hard so I didn't pee on the seats with happiness.

Later, though, we were just waiting around for something, I guess…or someone. It seemed to go on forever and was very confusing.

I looked up at the three different-sized ladies and tried to figure out what they were thinking about. I'd been hoping for a treat or two and was even trying out my best puppy-dog eyes on the oldest one, but so far it hadn't worked.

The littlest person (her name is Jawjaw) was complaining and grumbling because she said I was going to mess up her room. What room? We were in the yard! At this point, my understanding of the Peoplish language was pretty crummy, but I could tell she wasn't happy with me. I wagged my tail and jumped up a few times, leaving muddy paw-prints on her knees (humans LOVE that), but she pushed me away, grunting.

This can't be it, I thought to myself. *It's just like the shelter. No one wants to play.*

But...one person did...

"Hey!" a boy's voice shouted from inside the house.

Mom-Lady called to it, and a skinny kid with messy hair and long, gangly legs

clomped out through the back door.

That was it! That was the moment I laid eyes on my pet human for the first time. It makes my tail go crazy just remembering it.

"Surprise!" shouted Mom-Lady.

"Is that...?" My pet human gasped. He looked completely shocked, like he'd just swallowed a hornet's nest.

"It's a dog!" Grandmoo said.

"Well, yeah," mumbled my pet human, "but does he...?"

Jawjaw grumbled about something again. I was beginning to think I didn't like her all that much. She certainly didn't like me.

"I mean, is he...*mine?*" my pet human asked.

"Yes," said Mom-Lady. "He's yours, Ruff."

RUFF! The best-best-BESTEST name in all the world.

Before I knew it, Ruff was down on the ground and I was planting as many slobbery licks on his cheek as I could. He smelled like junk food and broken rules, and his face tasted like mischief. I loved all of it. They say you never adore anything as much as your first pet, and I couldn't agree more.

Don't get me wrong—I'd known plenty of other humans back before I wound up in the dog shelter, but none of those were mine to keep.

Finally I had a buddy for life. Just look at him...

RAFE ~~KHATCHA~~DORIAN

RUFF CATCH-A-DOGGY-BONE

His full name is Ruff Catch-A-Doggy-Bone.
I know! What are the odds a human would
have such a poochish name!?!

He smiled down at me, and I jumped about his legs, nipping and bouncing and yipping. It's what us dogs call "The Happy Dance."

Hey...don't judge. I was having the time of my little life, and once you've finished this book, you'll be Happy-Dancing all over the place, I'll bet.

Anyway, just when I thought things couldn't get any better...any more

TERRIFICALLY WONDERFUL

Ruff said the two most magical words I think ever existed.

They're so powerful, these words can leave you wagging your tail for days.

Agh! I'm not sure I can even tell you what he said, it makes me so overexcited.

Okay…breathe, Junior.

Breathe in…

Breathe out…

Breathe in…

Breathe out…

Right, I'm ready.

Ruff looked down at me.

He smiled his goofy human smile, then patted me on the head, opened his mouth…and said it:

HE JUST SAID IT!

I swear, I could have exploded into a billion little doggy pieces at that moment. Someone was telling me I was a GOOD BOY!

So there it is... the beginning of my story. We're on page 21 and you're still here reading with me. I knew you would be. Great, isn't it? Well, there's plenty more to tell you, so don't go anywhere just yet.

My life with the Catch-A-Doggy-Bone family had finally begun, and it's all fun and games from here on out in our BRILLIANT home.

Come and see if you don't believe me...

Today...Friday:
The Catch-A-Doggy-Bone
Kennel

Okay...if I tell the story properly...like PROPERLY-PROPERLY...you stand to learn quite a lot from my BRILLIANT diary. I'd say every human in the world could use a few tips on how to live a little bit more like us pooches. After all, who's happier than a dog?

Think of this book as a MUTT MANUAL...

CANINE CLASS . . . DROOL SCHOOL . . . and you'll be enjoying a more SMELL-TASTIC life in no time.

Let's start with a wander around my home. It's not as big and grand as some of the enormous kennels over on the far side of town, but for the Catch-A-Doggy-Bone pack, it's just right.

Our family kennel is warm and cozy, and FULL of all the things a dog needs to get by—when you know where to look.

Now, if you're going to live just like a MASTERFUL MUTT, you need to learn all the coolest hiding places, things to sniff, spots to stash your snacks and toys (a pooch's life is not worth living without those), escape routes, and vantage points for barking at people walking through your neighborhood.

You name it, I'll teach you where to find it.

If your kennel is anything like mine, it'll be stuffed full of all these and more.

C'mon...I'll show you the best parts.

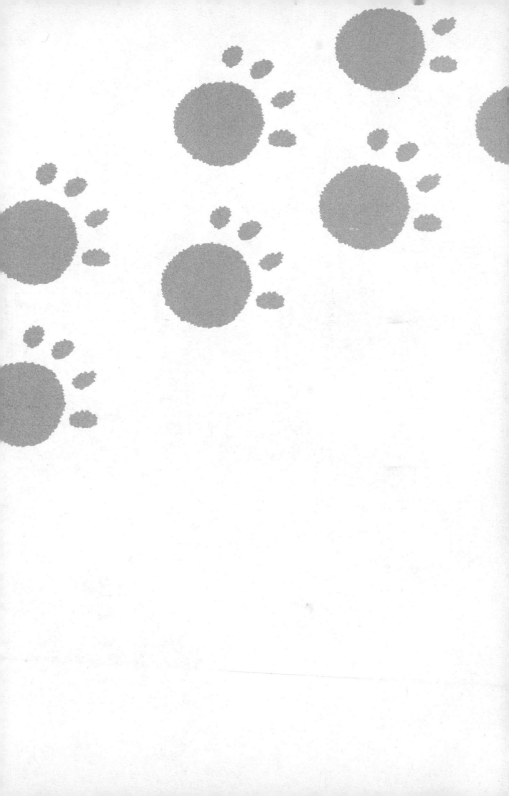

The Sleep Room

A pet human's sleep room is practically a jungle gym to us dogs. It's filled from top to bottom with amazing things to taste and smell and play with, and where all the best hugs and scratches happen. Let's not forget it's also the one place in the whole kennel where little brothers and sisters almost never dare to tread...almost. Treats hidden in here are safest from sniffing snouts and snooping eyes.

The Food Room

No human kennel is complete without a great big room filled with FOOD! It's the yummiest, smelliest, most snack-tastic place to be.

Just by luck, Mom-Lady keeps the broom in the same cupboard as all the bags and boxes of my treats.

I figured it out ages ago...the more mess I make, the more she opens the cupboard, giving me the chance to swipe a few

Crunchy-Lumps or Doggo-Drops. Ha ha! I'm a genius...what can I say?

Ah, food...I love you!

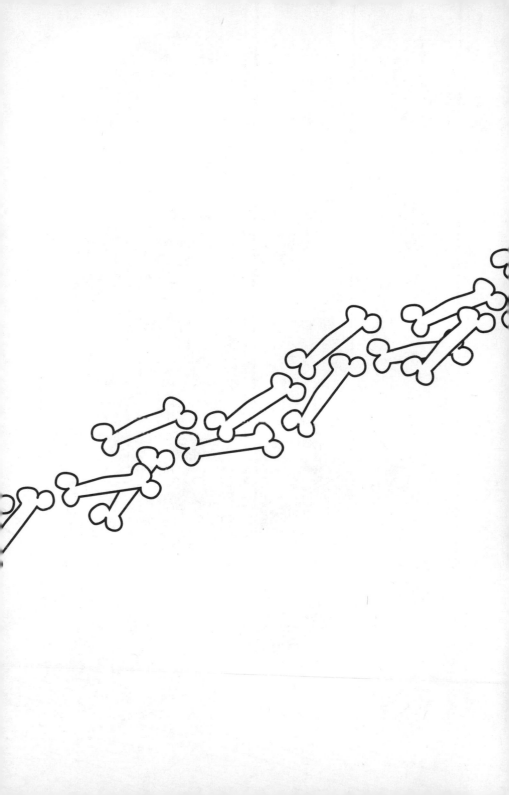

The Rainy Poop Room

This room is so weird! Whoever heard of a room just for pooping and washing? That's what backyards are for! Humans can be so funny at times...but hey...if you don't judge me for my Happy Dance, I won't judge you guys and your rainy poop rooms.

The Picture Box Room

The Picture Box Room is where humans love to sit and stare for hours. It's a real puzzle to me...

It's the one room of the kennel that has a perfect view of the street, which makes it a great barking base, and I keep my most delicious treats under the big hairy square on the floor. VERY IMPORTANT!

Jawjaw's Room

Jawjaw's Room is strictly out of bounds whenever she's at home, but the rooms you aren't supposed to go in are always the most interesting. Her shoes are by far the most delicious, but watch out for her army of mini-humans—they see everything!

The Backyard

The backyard is my little kingdom. It's extremely important that I protect it by barking at birds, squirrels, RACCOONS, airplanes, RACCOONS, clouds, neighbors, RACCOONS, and moving people-boxes on wheels...

AND RACCOONS!

Then there's one last place...

Brace yourself, my person-pal! I didn't want to have to show you this, but I have no choice. If your kennel is just like mine, there is one spot in your home that's more scary, more dangerous, MORE TERRI-FYING than any other.

Don't turn the page until you've hidden yourself safely away. GO!!

RUUUUUNNNNNNN!!!

Take my book with you and hide.

Under the bed! In the laundry pile! BEHIND THE COMFY SQUISHY THING!

Are you safe in your secret spot?

Okay...the most spine-jangling place in the house is...

Don't get me wrong, it's not the closet itself that's horrifying. It's what lives in there...

Lurking in the shadows among the coats and winter boots is a monster that would turn a Dalmatian's spots white with terror. It's my archest of enemies, and has gobbled up some of my most precious treasures in the past.

Inside that cupboard of doom lives...

THE VACUUM CLEANER!

It's the most evil creature I've ever met and it always comes out to roar around the house when Ruff and Jawjaw are at school. Mom-Lady pushes and pulls it through the rooms in a terrible battle of strength. It's hard to tell who's winning sometimes as it's sucking and slobbering up all the best pieces of breakfast from the floor, but eventually Mom-Lady always defeats it by unplugging its tail from the wall.

For instance—this morning, I'd spent ages gathering all my stashed treats and piling them together under the rug in the Picture Box Room. It was a mouthwatering masterpiece...and, you guessed it...just as I turned my back and headed off for a nap in Jawjaw's Room, the Vacuum Cleaner starts growling...then, *kapow!*

I barely made it to the Picture Box Room

door before that monster had gulped up my entire store. It was heartbreaking. I hid under Ruff's bed and whimpered to myself for hours after that.

He only managed to coax me out this evening with the promise of a fresh Denta-Toothy-Chew and one of his AMAZING belly rubs...

10 p.m.

Well, now you've learned all about the ins and outs of the Catch-A-Doggy-Bone kennel, I feel like we're really getting to know each other.

Ruff brought a big bowl of Tripple-Yummo-Banana-Twist ice cream to bed with him tonight, and now I'm curled up by his feet, watching him eat it as he doodles in his doo-dle pad.

My pet loves to draw. He's even drawn
me a few times.

I'm just going to keep quiet for now,
though, and let Ruff finish his ice cream. He
normally dozes off pretty soon after...
Then I can lick the bowl. HA HA!

Saturday

6:12 a.m.

Wake up! Wake up! Wake up!

Today is one of the two special days per week when Ruff doesn't go to school. They're my favorite! I get to spend two whole days with my best pet-pal and we can do whatever we want…and I mean anything!

I've had a good think about all the fun stuff I want to tick off the list, but it's so difficult to choose what to do first.

I definitely want to try out some new napping spots around the kennel, and of course I have to wait for the mailman to come (he loves it when I bark at him from the Picture Box Room window), and there's an unchewed table leg in the Food Room that I've been meaning to take care of for weeks.

A dog's work is never done...

I guess I should wake up Ruff. Normally I do it as soon as the sun rises (he LOVES it when I do that), but I let him sleep in a little later today. I'll just go stand on his face for a second.

Every good dog knows there's no nicer way for a human to be woken than with a paw-poke in the center of their forehead.

I'll just be a sec...

10 a.m.

And we're off, my person-pal...

After a quick game of bite-the-sock while Ruff was getting dressed, our usual breakfast of waffles and maple syrup for the humans and a bowl of CANINE CRISPY CRACKERS for me, we finally decided to go to the dog park.

It's one of the best things about mornings in the Catch-A-Doggy-Bone kennel.

We have a very set routine...

1. Ruff goes to the hallway closet to grab my leash, while I growl from a safe distance to let the Vacuum Cleaner know it can't make a dash for my other secret snack stashes around the kennel.

2. Ruff stands in the middle of the hallway, holding my leash, and I do the Happy Dance around his feet. This part is VERY important.

3. Once the performance is finished, I let Ruff connect the leash to my collar and I give it a few safety chews, just to make sure it's on there correctly.

4. Ruff opens the kennel door and I check
the coast is clear of RACCOONS!

5. LET THE WALK BEGIN!

I should tell you that I NEVER go out without my leash on. That way I know my pet human is holding tight and won't get lost when I'm leading him about. I've heard horror stories of careless dogs losing their person-pals and having to bark all over town just to find them. It's awful!

So, only once I know Ruff is safely attached on the other end of my leash do I allow him to head off through the neighborhood.

It's very important that I investigate every-body we pass with a quick jump-up to leave my paw-prints on their knees. It's my stamp of approval. That way, they know I've given them my permission and they're allowed on our street.

Oh…and there are all the SUPER-SERIOUS SNIFFING SPOTS we have to visit on the way. OBVIOUSLY!

10:28 a.m.

I can't wait to show you around the park, my furless friend. It's one of the best places in all of Hills Village, and for a super-good reason...

IT'S HOWL-TASTIC!

It's the perfect pooch playground, full of opportunities to cause a bit of chaos, meet your pooch-pals, and make loads of noise.

Yep...once you've peed on the gate, you can head inside the park knowing you're about to have the time of your life in the NOISIEST, SNIFFLEST, GO-CATCH-A-FRISBEE-EST place you'll find for miles and miles around.

There are dogs and their pet humans everywhere!

Fountains to run in and out of...The most talented dogs can run back and forth through the water jets without getting even a teensy bit wet!

The bushes are filled with hundreds of lost tennis balls from past games of Fetch that went wrong, and the grass is stuffed full of dropped treats from the doggy obedience classes that happen every evening. Ha! Whoever heard of an obedient dog?

The sticks are the stickiest you've EVER seen, and there are more pigeons than you could ever chase in a squillion years.

All in all, I'd say Hills Village Park is just about the most fun place you could hope to visit, and it's made even more AMAZING when my friends are also out taking their humans for WALKS.

My pooch-pack is awesome...

Don't get me wrong, people-pals are the most tremendous thing a dog could wish for, but you can't get by without some furry friends, too.

62

Allow me to introduce...

DIEGO

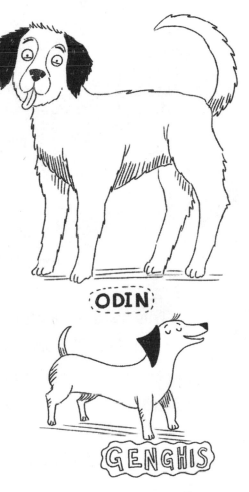

ODIN

BETTY

GENGHIS

This raggle-taggle bunch are my best-best-BESTEST pooch-pals. They're my sniffing squad! My Barking Bunch! MY PLAYTIME PACK!

HA!

A Quick History of Us...

These guys and I have been through a whole lot together. We met all the way back in our days at the Hills Village Dog Shelter. It was the six of us in one pen for what seemed like forever.

On those long days when things were at their bleakest and a bowl of Meaty-Giblet-Jumble-Chum seemed a lifetime away, we always took care of each other. It was in that horrible place that we swore...

Then one day, a kind-faced lady with more treats in her pockets than we could have imagined in our wildest dreams came and adopted Odin and Diego. They'd been together since they were pups, and somehow had still not figured out they weren't brothers. But, hey...they believed it, and no one had the heart to tell them there wasn't much of a family resemblance.

Sure enough, once Odin and Diego were saved, one by one all my cellmates were, too. Lola went next, followed by Genghis, then Betty, until I was the only loser left in that miserable prison. I remember crying myself to sleep at night, thinking nobody would ever want me and I'd never see any of my friends again. It was horrible!

Fast-forward to six months later. I was feeling about as gloomy and dejected as a mutt could be, so you can imagine my shock and delight when Mom-Lady came to pick me up.

Finally, I remember thinking to myself. *Finally, my luck has changed.* I'd never been so happy, and thought my life couldn't possibly get any better...until the day Ruff brought me to the park.

I was a little nervous. I hadn't been around this many dogs before, without metal bars separating us, and seeing so many of them bounding about made me miss my furry friends so much it hurt my heart.

Anyway, to cut a long story short, Ruff and I had only just made it out onto the playing field for a game of fetch when a wiry chihuahua trotted across my path.

My doggy eyes nearly jumped out of my head with surprise. I couldn't believe what I was seeing!

All the hairs on the back of my neck prickled on end as Diego froze in his tracks. He sniffed the air then spun around in my direction.

For a second we both just stared, until...

"MI AMIGO!" he barked.

He practically flew at my face and swung on my left ear. Then we rolled around in the grass, yipping and nipping at each other.

"Mi amigo!" he kept yelping as he play-bit me on my snout. "My old friend, returned?!?!"

My tail was swishing from side to side so fast I nearly batted the poor little guy across the field like a four-legged baseball.

Next thing I knew, Diego arched his spine, lifted his head, and HOOOOOOOWLED!

"HOOOOOOOOOWWWWLLLLLL!" came another voice from the other side of the field.

"OOOOW-OOOOWOOOOOOOOW!"
a third voice wailed from the fountains.

"BAAAA-WUUUUUUHHHHHH!"

"YIP-YIP-YIIIIIIIIIIIIIIIIIIIP!"

And that was that—I turned around slowly
to see all my best pooch-pals running toward
me from all different directions.

Needless to say...IT WAS A GOOD DAY!

There's not a whole lot I can say that properly describes just how great these guys are.

Odin and Diego are endlessly funny. You should see it when Diego scampers beneath something low, like a trash can or a bench, and Odin can't figure out why he's not able to make it under like his brother...ha ha!

Lola lives to roll in mud. She's more hippopotamus than dog, I think. A French bull-hippo.

Genghis loves to run between your legs and steal the tennis ball you were just playing with right out from under your nose, and Betty is a master of canine comedy. She really is!

Sometimes I wish Ruff spoke Doglish. I find it easy to understand Peoplish and what my pet has to say, but humans just aren't as smart as dogs, sadly.

If Ruff could understand Betty, he'd be rolling about in the grass with us, laughing his two legs off.

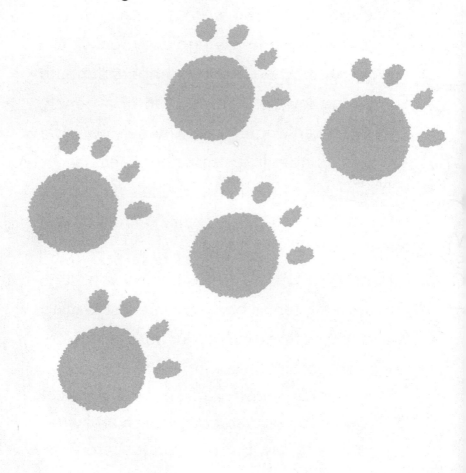

Which kind of dog would keep a vampire as a pet?
A bloodhound!
What do you call a magical dog?
A labracadabra!
Did you hear a cat won the dog show?
It was a cat-has-trophy!
A Scottie ran into a monster.... he was terrier-fied!

11:45 a.m.

THIS IS A DISASTER! Oh no, my person-pal!! There has been a terrible incident. It was so BAD I think I might have gotten Ruff and me into more trouble than we've ever been in before.

My heart is racing so much I can hardly speak. I think I might need to lie down!

No! Come on, Junior. You can do this.

Well, my furless friend, we were just hanging around in the park, having an AMAZING time, when...

I SAW IT!

I caught a flash of gray and black as something small and furry ran between the trash cans and the jungle gym.

My ears pricked up and my super-sniff-a-licious nose caught the garbagy whiff of rac...rac...

That was it! I couldn't help myself. Before Ruff could stop me, I bolted across the playing field, barking my extra-barkiest bark that I save just for rac...rac...RAC...RAAAAC...RACCOONS!

I don't know what it is about them that drives me so CRAZY!

Just seeing their stripy tails sends me into a frenzy. Chasing and barking at them is one of my favorite hobbies in the world. It's just so much fun!

I suppose if I had only run after it and barked, things wouldn't have been so bad. The problem is, when a dog sees another dog racing across open grass, they just HAVE to follow. IT'S IRRESISTIBLE!

In no time I was pelting across the park with every single dog who was there today, all following me.

Of course that doesn't sound too bad, I know.

So what if all the dogs ran over to the jungle gym? It's no big deal, right?

Well...ummmm...it didn't quite end there.

A Saint Bernard named Tallulah who joined in the chase had been tied to a drinking fountain outside the public restrooms.

In all the excitement of my little scene, she pulled the thing off the wall, sending a huge arc of water crashing onto some unsuspecting grandmoos on a bench opposite.

Another dog had his leash knotted to the stroller his pet human was pushing, and before she knew what was happening, the lady was screaming at the top of her lungs as her baby was hurtling backward across the park, being towed by an overexcited Akita named Dwayne.

It was canine carnage!

Picnics were trampled, toddlers were toppled, and the peace of the park was most definitely shattered.

To top things off, as we all clattered about the jungle gym looking for the rac...rac— oh, you know what I'm trying to say—a stern-looking woman in a green uniform marched into the middle of the chaos and lunged at me.

I ducked under her outstretched arm, then bolted between her legs before she could get her hands on my collar. Who did she think she was, trying to stop my raccoon chase?

"COME HERE!" she bellowed at me, spinning around to make a second grab.

Now everything got even more wild. If there's one thing that makes dogs run wild more than when they're chasing something, it's when they're being chased.

"BAD DOG!" the woman yelled, diving out of the path of the high-speed stroller as it careened behind Dwayne.

Bad dog? Was she talking to me?!?! I was just doing some very important barking—what's wrong with that?

Before I knew it, the woman was in speedy pursuit. She was screaming and sweating, and I'm not ashamed to admit it, but I started to panic.

"GET BACK HERE!" The angry lady pulled a whistle from her pocket and blew it. "WHO OWNS THIS DOG?"

I'm not entirely sure what happened next. My pooch instincts kicked into gear and all I could think about was getting away from the strange human who'd called me a...a...BAD DOG!

Those are two of the most rotten words. Worse than swearing!

"BAD DOG" means no treats. It means being shut out in the yard, or sent to your bed without any dinner. Those two words mean you'll eventually wind up back in the Hills Village Dog Shelter.

Suddenly, in all the howling and yelling and grabbing, I heard Ruff's voice. He was calling my name, which was like a tiny explosion of happiness in my heart, but I couldn't stop now. The angry whistle-lady had nearly caught up with me, and I wasn't about to let myself be grabbed by her.

So…I'm sure you're wondering what happened in the end. Did I find the raccoon? Did the crazy woman catch me and throw me in pooch prison to spend the rest of my days locked away, until there is nothing left in my cage except a pile of bones?

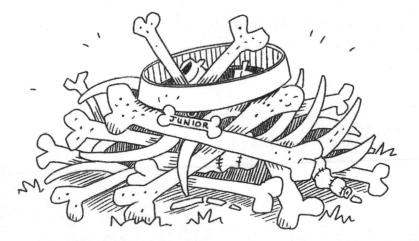

Brace yourself, my furless friend. What I'm about to tell you is worse than all of those things. SO MUCH WORSE! If you had a tail, this next part of my diary would make it curly with shock.

Picture it...

There's chaos! All of us dogs were barking our raccoon warnings and scrabbling about the place, and the humans were yelling at their dog-owners in return. And right in the middle of all of this is Whistling Wilma, swatting this way and that. My heart was beating faster and faster and FASTER, until...

Silence.

It took a moment for me to even notice that everyone, four-legged and two-legged alike, had just stopped in their tracks and was staring over at the swing set.

"Junior! What have you done?" It was

Ruff's voice coming from a little way off, behind me.

I spun around and…HA! I couldn't help but laugh. In all our twisting and turning, the crazy whistle-lady had gotten herself knotted up in the ropes of the swing and was dangling like an enormous ball of human yarn just above the ground.

What did she expect? No one can outrun
JUNIOR-TRON 5000!!

"P'toooey!" She spat the whistle out of
her mouth and glared at the crowd of people
that had gathered. "GET ME DOWN FROM
HERE!"

"Ma'am, I'm so sorry," Ruff said. He
darted over to the swings and started trying
to untwist the red-faced woman.

"I MEAN IT!" she snapped at Ruff as he
pulled at a piece of rope that was looped
around her belly. "UNTANGLE ME!"

"Yes, ma'am."

"NOW!!!"

My human pet gave one last almighty
yank on the tattered end of the swing-rope
and the crazy lady flopped onto the ground
with a very winded "OOOOOOOOFF!"

Nobody made a sound.

I watched nervously as she flapped about on her side before stumbling to her feet.

"You!" the woman hissed, almost pressing her nose right against Ruff's. "Are you the owner of this unruly mongrel?"

She jabbed a finger in my direction without moving her eyes away from my pet human.

Mongrel? Who was she calling a mongrel? I'm all the best parts of tons of different dog breeds all rolled into one. I'M A CANINE COCKTAIL!

"Umm...y-yes...he's my dog," Ruff said. "Look, I'm sorry—"

"Oh, save your 'I'm sorrys' for somebody else. That mutt is practically wild! Look at the chaos he's caused." She gestured her arm around the park and it was the first time I noticed the mess we'd all made...well...I'd made. "Do you know who I am?"

"No," Ruff said.

"Nope," I barked, but she didn't under-stand me.

The lady took a little card from a pouch on her belt and handed it to Ruff.

The Perfect ~Pooch~
Obedience training for dogs

"My name is Iona Stricker," she said.

Both my pet and I jolted with surprise. I knew that human surname! It was the same as the MONSTER who bullied her way around Hills Village Middle School. "Ida Stricker...QUEEN OF DETENTION!" That's what Ruff used to call her. He'd grumble to me about that grouchy old lady all the time, without realizing I understood every word he was saying.

"S-S-Stricker?" Ruff stammered.

"Yes."

"Like...Ida Stricker?"

"That's Principal Stricker to you, young man...but yes, Ida Stricker is my aunt."

Ruff opened his mouth to speak, then closed it, then opened it...I'd never seen my pet human looking so confused and stressed.

"Anyway," the lady said, "I run the obedience classes here at Hills Village Park. I don't think I've ever seen a dog that needs them more."

"No...you don't understand," Ruff tried to explain, but Cranky-Pants Stricker grunted.

"Wrong!" she snapped. "It is you who doesn't understand."

She turned and glared at me for the first time, and before I could stop myself, a low growl rumbled out of my throat.

"This creature is a nuisance, a blight, an embarrassment to the park," Stricker said, pointing at me again. "If you do not enroll yourself and your dog in my intensive best-behavior course immediately, I'll be forced to report him to the Hills Village Dog Shelter and have him taken away."

11:57 a.m.

I can't do it, my furless friend.

I...I...I'll never survive obedience classes. I just know it!

How can a dog like me spend all those hours running this way and that, listening to Iona "Whistle Pants"

Stricker jabber on when there's serious sniffing to be done?

Who's going to guard the kennel from the Vacuum Cleaner, or separate the pairs of socks and bury one of each color in the backyard?

Who's going to bark at the mailman in the morning? He'll be devastated if he doesn't receive his special greeting!

WHO'S GOING TO WAKE UP RUFF AT SUNRISE WITH A LOVING PAW-POKE!?!

This is the worst day in the history of the universe...EVER!!

I'm a goner, I can feel it.

Boredom is going to rot my brains and I'll be heading up to that great kennel in the sky any day now.

Good-bye, cruel world. Good-bye!!

The Last Will and Testament of Junior Catch-A-Doggy-Bone

Dearest friends of the four-legged and two-legged variety,

If you are reading this, it means I shriveled up and bit the duster at the unimaginable shock and horror of having to attend The Perfect Pooch obedience training. I hereby leave my precious possessions as follows:

1. Ruff, I want you to have my collection of prize sticks that I hid in the back of your closet under your old T-shirt with the paint stains on it.

2. Mom-Lady can have the half-peeled tennis ball I keep buried down the side of the cushions on the comfy squishy thing.

3. Grandmoo can have my water-bowl—even better for drinking from than the toilet.

4. Jawjaw is allowed to keep the poop I left in her phys ed sneakers. You're welcome.

5. Odin and Diego, to you I leave all my Canine Crispy Crackers. The best doggy treats in all the world.

6. Lola gets my Denta-Toothy-Chews. May they keep your teeth strong and plaque-free forevermore.

7. Genghis can have my cans of Crunchy-Lumps. Don't eat them all at once.

8. Betty can take the big bag of Doggo-Drops—one for every joke you ever told me.

9. Oh, and whenever someone gets a moment, please pee (and/or poop) on Iona Stricker's doorstep as much as possible.

Yours sincerely,

Dead Junior

8:30 p.m.

Okay...so I may have overreacted a little, but that was a pretty nasty surprise for a little mutt like me to have, no?

Did you survive the terrible shock, my person-pal?

Tell me you're still here and haven't sunk into a pit of hopelessness, screaming "IT'S TOO AWFUL!"

Don't despair just yet. I know it looks as though things couldn't get any worse right now, and the idea of having to go to Iona Stricker's boring, brain-numbing, dull and dreary, humdrum, horrible LECTUROUS LESSONS seems like a fate worse than death, but hey...they don't call me "Crafty McSmart, the Cleverest Canine" for nothing.

Okay...no one has ever called me that ... EVER...but I'm as sharp as they come and I've got a plan.

After the INSANE WHISTLE-LADY flounced off, Ruff and I plodded home in silence. It was terrible! I felt so guilty for my poor human pet. He'd have to go through all the pain and sorrow of obedience classes, too, because of me.

BUT...every kibble bowl has a silver lining.

Before long, the two of us snuggled up on the comfy squishy thing in the Picture Box

95

Room, and Ruff opened a jumbo pack of SIZZLE-CHICK'N-POTATO-CHIPS.

I gotta say…most human food is pretty bland. A lot of it doesn't even have giblets in it! But OH BOY, do I love potato chips.

I don't know which part of a chicken it is that potato chips come from, but it's the BEST part for sure.

I always get my best ideas when I'm curled up with Ruff eating snacks and looking at the picture box, and in no time a BRILLIANT, TERRIFIC, BRAINYBONKING plan popped into my head.

It's simple really.

Ready to hear it?

Okay…

I'll just ace the class!!

TA-DAA! I told you it was BRILLIANT. I can't believe I didn't think of it sooner.

I'm such a super-smart dog...well...I think...no, I KNOW! What can be so difficult about sitting, begging, rolling over, and all that useless stuff?

I'll wander down to old Stricker's obedience school with Ruff tomorrow and we'll graduate in ten minutes. EASY!

Sunday

8:16 a.m.

Up bright and early for a little bit of practicing on my own, ready to show the world just how easy obedience can be.

Now, in case you didn't know what obedience means—it's a strange human game of make-believe where the person pretends they are the owner, and their dog is the pet. I know... it's super weird!

The idea of the game is to impress your human so much with a kind of dance of sitting down, lying flat, staying put, and rolling over, that they give you a squillion treats.

From what I've heard, the human will bark lots of commands in a serious voice.

Now, my understanding of the Peoplish language is obviously great, but sadly I never bothered to learn all those types of command words.

I'm not worried though. I'm pretty sure it doesn't really matter what command your pet human is saying, as long as you do all your best moves...and BOY, DO I HAVE SOME GOOD MOVES!

There's no way I won't be top of the class! I'm going to be swimming in snacks at Stricker's classes. HA HA!

9:07 a.m.

I'm starting with all the basics in the back-yard. Ruff is indoors practicing a few of his command words, while I'm perfecting all the amazing stuff I can do.

It should be as easy as napping—I've seen this stuff on the picture box billions of times.

10 a.m.

We're here, my furless friend...back at Hills Village Park, and it's looking like obedience class is super busy today. I'm raring to show old Prissy-Pants Stricker how wrong she was about me.

I'll prove I'm no embarrassment, or nuisance, or whatever it was she called me...I wasn't really listening.

> Good morning, dog owners and your canine companions. Ahead of you lies a day of grueling, difficult, and taxing training that will transform your pets from misbehaved mutts into sophisticated servants.

10:03 a.m.

Here we go...
    Servants?
She's loop-the-loop
crazy! Whoever heard of a
dog serving its human? Ha ha!

Let's get this over and done
with, my person-pal.

104

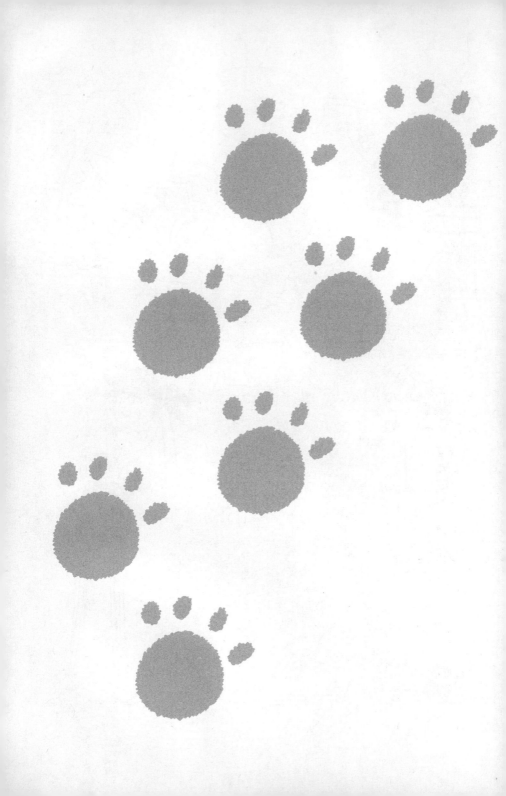

3:56 p.m.

Phew! We're done, my furless friend...I was amazing! While all the other dogs were doing the same old tricks, I showed off some incredible doggy skills.

There were moments when Miss Stricker was staring at me with eyes as big as kibble bowls and her mouth hanging wide open. If that isn't a look of complete amazement, I don't know what is.

We're having the graduation ceremony on

the bandstand in just a few minutes. I can't wait to see all their faces when I'm awarded TOP OF THE CLASS. Ruff will be so proud of me, I can just feel it!

I'll let you know how it goes…

4:15 p.m.

STOP EVERYTHING!
THE WORLD HAS GONE MAD!
IT'S COMPLETELY BONKERS!!
IT'S HAD ITS BRAIN SCRAMBLED!!!

I don't know what happened, my person-pal.
It's all gone wrong. My perfect plan failed and
I...ugh! I can't bring myself to even say it.

   I...I...OH, JUST LOOK AT THE

GRADUATION PHOTO.

THE PERFECT POOCH
INTENSIVE OBEDIENCE COURSE

We failed! Ruff and I are the BIGGEST LOSERS in the whole class and that means... OH NO!

8 p.m.

I really don't know where to start. This has been a serious evening for the books, let me tell you.

So...last time we spoke, Ruff and I had just failed STUPID STRICKER'S STUPID, STU-PID, STUUUUPID SCHOOL!

Ruff tried to reason with her, but that whistling old whiner was having none of it.

They argued for ages, but nothing Ruff said could convince that RABID RODENT to change her mind.

I could almost smell the disgusting whiff of the gross meat-free dog food they feed the inmates at Hills Village Dog Shelter. It's puke-a-licious!!

What was I going to do?

I couldn't go back there!

But THAT was when things got interesting...

I'm ashamed to admit it, but after I saw how helpless and sad Ruff looked with Stricker yelling at him, I was about ready to give up.

I was whimpering to myself, hanging my head, and figuring that Ruff might just be better off without me, when I spotted it...

There, trampled into the mud by a gazillion

feet and paws, was a paper flyer.

At first I glanced straight past it. Who cares about a flyer in the dirt at a time like this, right?

Now, I may be able to understand Peoplish speak more than most dogs, but I'm no reader. Human writing is strange and twisty and downright confusing to us canines, but one word across the top of it caught my eye.

There was a "D," and an "O," and a "G" . . .

I knew that word. It's written on all the boxes of kibble that Mom-Lady keeps next to the broom in the Food Room cupboard. It spells "DOG."

I scraped my paw across it and uncovered more of the flyer.

There was a picture of the happiest pooch I think I'd ever seen. He was being lifted into the air by his pet human and between them was an enormous trophy.

A trophy?

I snatched up the flyer in my jaws and ran to Ruff's feet.

At first Ruff just ignored me as I poked and scraped at his ankle to get attention. He was still busy being yelled at by Stricker, so I can't say I blame him.

I put the flyer on his shoe and tried tugging at Ruff's jeans with my teeth, but he still didn't look down at me.

I yanked on his laces and head-poked his shins. I even sniffed his butt to see if that would make a difference... It didn't.

There was only one thing for it. Desperate times call for desperate measures, so I...

Okay, okay, okay...I know that was a revolting thing to subject your pet to when he's trying to save you from being thrown back into pooch prison, but what else was I supposed to do?

And anyway...it did the trick...HA HA!

Ruff let out a cry of disbelief and gaped down at me. He made a swipe to catch me by the collar but I was WAY quicker. As he reached down toward me, I snatched up the crumpled flyer and stuffed it into my pet's hand...And the rest, as they say, is history.

8:45 p.m.

As you can probably guess, I'm not back at the shelter yet, my person-pal. NOT EVEN CLOSE!

Right now, Ruff and I are curled up on the comfy squishy thing, watching *Zombie Apocalympics* on the picture box. It's one of Ruff's favorite

moving pictures to watch.

Ha ha! Don't panic! Don't start flapping about like a demented rooster!! I'm going to tell you what happened earlier.

After I stuffed the flyer into his hand, Ruff took one look at it and gasped.

"A dog show!"

"So what?" Stricker scoffed in his face.

"We'll enter!"

"You and that mutt?" she laughed. "In the Debonair Dandy-Dog Show?!"

"Yes!" said Ruff. "We'll enter!"

"And?"

"If we win a prize, you can't report Junior to Hills Village Dog Shelter."

Stricker smiled a vinegary smile.

"You foolish boy," she hissed. "The Dandy-Dog Show is only one week away.

You think someone as unruly as you could ever train up a rotten beast in time to...to...WIN A PRIZE?" She burst out laughing.

"Yes! It says here there's a BASIC BEGIN-NERS round. We could win that...I know we could."

"Nonsense!"

"What's the matter, Mrs. Stricker?" Ruff said with a grin. "Scared I'll prove you wrong, like I did your aunt?"

Stricker's face turned bright red and her head looked like it might rocket off her shoulders.

"That's PRINCIPAL AUNT to you!" she barked. Then her face fell into an angry frown. "Fine! You have one week...and when you lose in every category, I'm going to have that mangy mongrel locked away for good."

"Fine!" Ruff snapped back at her.

Stricker turned to go, but just before she marched off across the park, she stopped and said...

"I'd be very worried if I were you, Mr. Khatchadorian."

I nearly laughed in her face. That's not how you pronounce Catch-A-Doggy-Bone!

"I shall be entering my own dog, Duchess, into the Basic Beginners round..." Stricker continued. "And Duchy-Poo wins everything!"

She grinned like someone sucking on a lemon, then placed the whistle that hung around her neck to her crusty lips and blew a long *PEEEEEEEEEEEEEEEEEEEP!* on it.

In no time at all, the most perfectly poised poodle I've ever seen trotted over from somewhere behind the flowerbeds and sat in front of Stricker like a curly-haired robot.

I'd never seen anything like it. She didn't scratch or sniff the air or even beg for a treat!!

HELLO?!? I was only a few feet away and she didn't even glance at me once. What kind of pooch sees another dog for the first time and doesn't even give it a good sniff?

"As I was saying," Stricker continued, "you don't stand a chance of beating Duchess."

With that, the sour-faced woman performed a series of hand gestures and her poodle-princess leaped into a display of the tidiest, most perfect rolls and twists and jumps. She even twirled about on her hind legs like a human.

I couldn't help but be impressed by Stricker and her curly-haired canine. Maybe the woman was right—maybe we didn't stand a chance? I'm not sure I could do any of the amazing tricks I'd just witnessed.

I looked up at Ruff and saw that his face had turned as pale as one of my Denta-Toothy-Chews.

"Well..." he blurted, "if...if your dog is so good, why are you entering her into the Basic Beginners round?"

"That's only a warm-up to us," Stricker said, sneering. "Winning is no fun unless you win EVERYTHING! We plan to take home every trophy there is, and you and your mangy mutt won't stop us."

It was at that moment that Duchess looked at me for the first time, and it's hard to tell with all that curly fur, but I would swear

130

she was sneering just like her pet human...

AND THAT WAS THAT! Stricker and her POOP-dle flounced off, and we headed home.

Sooooo...Ruff has gotten us the second chance we needed. Now all we have to do is win a trophy at the dog show next weekend.

How hard can it be? I mean...I know we got pretty much everything wrong in the obedience class, and I got the lowest score ever from any dog that attended it...but I'm optimistic...I think...

Monday

Training Day 1!!

4 p.m.

Ruff ran straight home from school and we're in the backyard ready to perfect our dog-to-human synchronicity.

I think that's what they called it…

Late last night, Ruff found some moving picture clips of these dog show thingies on his compu-za-ma-wazit. It doesn't look too difficult...just lots of doing weird stuff for treats.

He says we're going to enter the Basic Beginners round.

In case you didn't know, "Basic" is the human word for really, really, really AMAZING...and "Beginners" means the most talented dogs.

Naturally, I'm certain we'll ace it. It can't go wrong twice in a row, huh?

Okay, let's figure this out...

OH, MY WAGGY TAIL, I JUST GOT IT!!

Are you telling me, after all this time, I only had to listen to my pet human and actually do what he asked to graduate obedience class?!?!?

WHY DIDN'T YOU SAY SO?

THIS IS A REVELATION!!!!

Tuesday

4 p.m.

This is so EASY, a pup could do it! WHO KNEW!?!

Wednesday

4:30 p.m.

SIMPLE!

Ha ha! Just kidding!

6:28 p.m.

Hold everything...something really weird is going on, person-pal!

After our TREMENDOUS training session in the backyard, Ruff and I headed inside the kennel, ready for our dinner.

While Ruff stopped to talk to Mom-Lady in the Food Room, I quickly trotted off to the Sleep Room to dig out an extra-tasty bone I'd been hiding in the laundry pile for ages. I've been saving it for a special occasion and today felt like the right day to feast on it.

So...I was carrying my bone back down the hall to the Food Room when I heard Mom-Lady talking to Ruff in her serious voice.

SERIOUS VOICE? She should be using her happy voice! Ruff and I were going to ACE the dog show.

I crept to the door and listened. At first I couldn't understand what she was talking to Ruff about, but then...then...I heard her say one of the scariest words in the whole universe.

It's a TERRIBLE, UGLY word that makes my fur stand on end and my stomach gurgle with nervousness.

Mom-Lady said the V word...

v...v...vet!!!

What was going on?! I thought I'd been a good boy? Why would Mom-Lady want to punish me by taking me to the v...v...VET CLINIC?!

That's not all...She was planning for the veterinarian to...to...

MICROCHIPPED? I don't want to be turned into micro chips!

How could Mom-Lady do this? Why would she do it?

In all my doggy nightmares I NEVER imagined I'd end up being cut up into tiny little crispy pieces and put in foil bags for humans to snack on!!!! What if it hurts? WHAT IF I END UP SOUR CREAM AND ONION FLAVOR?

8:45 p.m.

Okay...so I may have gotten a little bit carried away. After hearing the awful news that Mom-Lady was planning to turn me into a crispy snack, I pooped in her sneakers by the front door and went to cower under Ruff's bed.

I was devastated, and it didn't take Ruff long to figure out that something was seriously wrong.

145

He kept trying to coax me out with hand-fuls of Oinky-Pig-Puffs but I wasn't going to be caught that easily. I couldn't figure out why he was so calm. He should be sobbing and pooping in every shoe he could find! Didn't he care that his BESTEST pooch-pal in the whole world was going to be chipped?

After a few hours of extra-whimpery whim-pering, my stomach finally got the better of me and I crawled out to eat the now massive pile of treats.

If I was going to be chopped up into little pieces, I might as well enjoy one last feast, right?

Anyway...I had gotten it all wrong. After I'd quietly eaten all the food Ruff had put by the bed for me, he scooped me up and we sat down together to watch *Robo-Bandits* on the picture box. It's one of our favorites usually.

I wasn't really watching until I heard that word again and pricked up my ears.

How could I be so stupid? Mom-Lady wasn't talking about potato chips! She was talking about having me turned into a crime-fighting robot dog, which sounds… which sounds…AMAZING!!!

I'll be the coolest dog in the whole of Hills Village and able to beat Stricker and Duchess with my amazing new robo-bilities.

Just think of it, my person-pal!

Now, I don't know exactly what the outcome of getting microchipped is, but I bet it's going to look something like this…

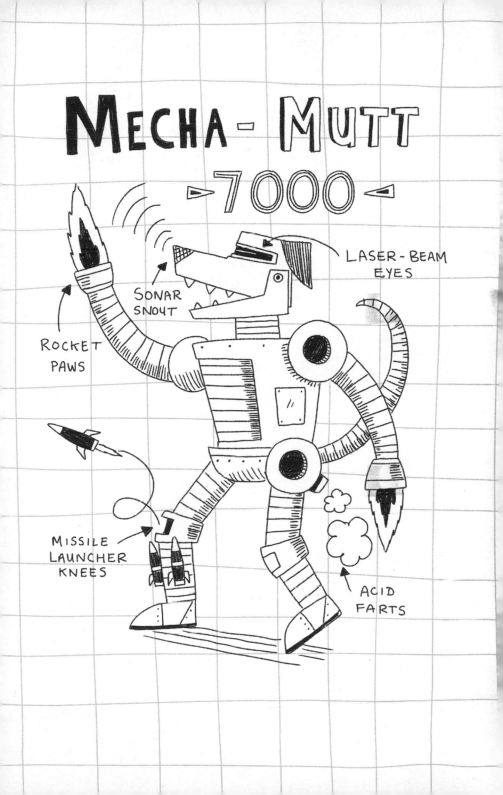

Things have taken a real turn for the better. This must be the first time I've EVER been excited to visit the vet clinic in my life. HA!

Right, I'd better get to bed. The faster I'm asleep, the faster I'll be a mechanical slobber-tron. AAAAGH! I can't wait!!

Thursday

9:08 a.m.

Here we go, my furless friend. Ruff has left the kennel for school and Mom-Lady and I are in the moving people-box on wheels, heading to the veterinarian. I'm so excited I want to stick my head out the window and howl!

9:37 a.m.

We're here! Agh! I can't believe this is actually happening. All I can do is think about how happy it'll make Ruff to be the pet of a real-life robo-pooch. It's going to be TERRIFIC!

1 p.m.

Okay...that was a disappointment. It turns out that getting microchipped is pretty boring after all. It was just a weensy thing they stuck into the back of my neck with a tiny poking device. I barely felt a thing...And I haven't noticed any new robot powers.

Oh well, the vet was a friendly human lady who gave me a sausage stick for being a good boy, so it's not all bad, I guess.

I was so looking forward to blasting Stricker to smithereens with my laser-beam eyes, though...Hmph.

5 p.m.

This is all taking too long now! Come on, come on, come on!!

Laser-beam eyes or not, I can't wait to win the Basic (AMAZING) Beginners (TALENT) section and see Stricker's face when we beat her dog Duchess.

We just couldn't compete with Junior's incredible-ness!

Artist's Impression

Friday

8:45 p.m.

AAAAAAAGGGGHHHHH!!! I can't wait any longer!!

I'm so excited to go to the dog show, I think I might burst.

I don't know what to do with myself!

It's sooooo close I can almost...

Saturday

7:28 a.m.

Uhhh...I must have nodded off.

YAHOOOOOOO!!!

It's here, my person-pal! You stayed with me all the way through my day-to-day doggy diary and now we've finally reached the grand finale.

THE DEBONAIR DANDY-DOG SHOW!!

Now give me a little private time if you don't mind, old friend. I've gotta brave the drippy water box in the Rainy Poop Room so I can look as much like a DASHINGLY POLISHED POOCH as I can.

I'm not taking any chances...

8 a.m.

Hey...where'd all this extra fur come from?
And what's that strange smell?

Oh...that's what CLEAN smells like...

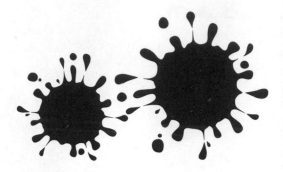

9:30 a.m.

WOW! I've never seen anything like this! The Debonair Dandy-Dog Show is MASSIVE! It's filled the whole of Hills Village Community Center and OH BOY are there some interesting smells drifting my way.

There are dogs and their pet humans everywhere and, for as far as my eyes can see, there are shops and stalls selling doggy fashion, beds, grooming kits, pictures, and CHEW TOYS!! I swear I just saw Lola and Genghis getting pooch pedicures!

And...DRUMROLL, PLEASE...there's even the world's largest can of Meaty-Giblet-Jumble-Chum, and people are having their pictures taken in front of it!! IT'S A CANINE CARNIVAL!

9:42 a.m.

This place is amazing! You should see it, my furless friend. I just led Ruff along a whole aisle of food stalls on our way to the competition ring and I could barely stop myself from drooling.

The human stalls were boring...

THE
LUNCH-PACK
OF
NOTRE DAME

GREAT
EGG-
SPECTATIONS

MUFFIN
TO
WORRY ABOUT

But there were special stalls just for dogs as well. Now those ones were anything but boring!

'TIL WE MEAT AGAIN

YOU'RE BACON ME CRAZY

THE WIENER TAKES IT ALL

LET'S TACO-BOUT IT

Note to self: Definitely stop back here after you're crowned the winner of the dog show...although steer clear of the hot dog stand. I'm not sure about that one. It smelled like...I can't put my paw on it...

9:53 a.m.

Ugh! It's so nearly time to impress the whole world with my great tricks, I'm struggling to keep my tail-wagging under control.

Just...so...exciting!

9:56 a.m.

And we're here...The Basic (Amazing) Beginners (Talent) category is competing in the Grand Competition Ring, right at the center of the dog show. It feels like the entire universe has turned up to watch.

Odin and Diego are competing, too. TRE-MENDOUS!

There's so much to take in, I can hardly believe what I'm seeing.

And look...I snatched a map from under someone's seat so you can see for yourself.

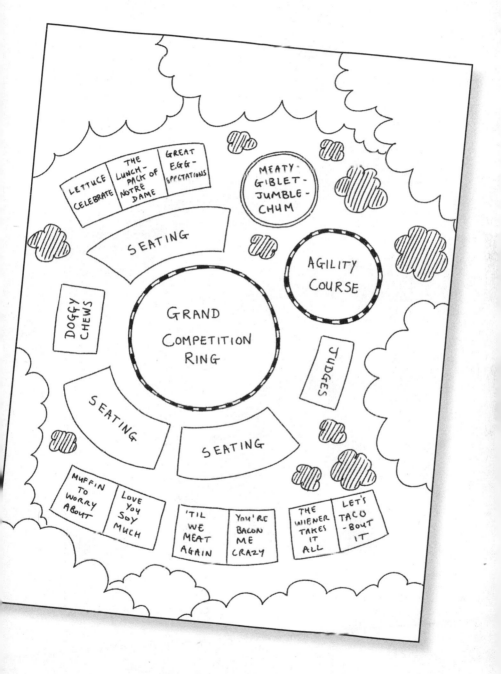

9:58 a.m.

Blarg! SMUG ALERT!! Look who's just shown up...

I swear I've never seen a more pompous pooch or pukish person-pet.

9:59 a.m.

Only one minute to go, my person-pal. It's been such a pleasure getting to know you, it really has.

Okay...wish me luck...I'll let you know how it goes on the other side...

11:47 a.m.

HA HA! THAT WAS AMAZING! You should have seen me, my person-pal. I AM THE CHAMPION!!

Okay...that's not completely true, but I'm a sort-of-champion and that's just as GOOD, if you ask me!

I'll explain...ten a.m. rolled around and all the dogs competing in the Basic (AMAZING)

Beginners (TALENT) category were invited into the Grand Competition Ring with their pet humans.

There were so many people crowded around the edges, I started to get more and more nervous, but the sight of Stricker and her haughty hound, Duchess, forced me to keep my cool.

I wasn't about to let those two win and wind up back at Hills Village Dog Shelter.

At first it started pretty simply. The judges gave commands to our pet humans from their table at the front, then—one by one—our pet humans gave the same command to us dogs, and we had to perform it.

No worries there.

We sat, we lay down, we rolled over,

we spun around in circles, and we fetched things...yada-yada-yada. Now that I understood I was supposed to do as I was told, it was all really easy...and...well...BORING!

I know what you're thinking. You're reading this and saying to yourself: "NO! JUNIOR! CONCENTRATE!"

Well, I hate to break it to you, my furless friend, my mind wandered and I messed up the Basic (AMAZING) Beginners (TALENT) trial BIG TIME...and...

I WAS STUPENDOUS!!

We were nearly finished and I was doing great. I have to hand it to Dainty Duchess and her pet, Stricker. That is one terrifically trained poodle, and they were doing super well, too—not quite as good as Ruff and me...but close.

Anyway, just as the last "play dead" test was coming up, I caught sight of the agility course over on the next competition ring from us.

It looked so much more fun than what we were doing.

Dogs were hurtling around what looked like a humongous JUNGLE GYM!

I remember thinking: *I wish I was over there with those guys.* That's when I looked down and noticed that I was running at breakneck speed.

I don't know what happened!!

You remember I talked about doggy instincts earlier in the book? Well, if there's one thing you should know about that kind of stuff, it's that WHEN YOU FEEL THE URGE TO RUN OFF IN SEARCH OF MORE FUN, YOU JUST GOTTA GO WITH IT!

I heard Ruff's voice yelling behind me, but there was nothing I could do to stop myself.

I tore out of the grand ring and raced through the crowds of people in the direction of ALL THAT FUN AND EXCITEMENT.

It was at about that moment, as I was darting between people's legs, I noticed Odin was careening alongside me, knocking busy humans flying in all directions. He was grinning and flopping his tongue from side to side, and Diego was hanging on for dear life from one of his big brother's ears.

A pang of happiness exploded in my belly. If I'd messed this all up and was going to be hauled back to pooch prison, it felt good to be doing it with my buddies in tow.

"MOVE!"

Something fluffy barged past and shoved me aside. I looked round in shock to see Duchess tearing past me.

"Freedom!" she howled over her shoulder as she reached the entrance to the agility ring. "AT LAST!"

Ha ha! I don't think I've ever had such a fun, rambunctious, noisy, run-abouty afternoon in all my doggy days.

As you
know…
if one dog
bolts across
open ground,
all dogs have to follow.

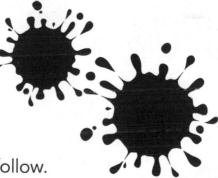

You should have seen the looks on some of the competitors' faces as thirty hysterically excited dogs flooded onto the agility course and started leaping all over the place.

It was POOCH-A-LICIOUS, my person-pal. IT WAS BARK-TASTIC!

The well-behaved-little-dog voice inside my head told me to stop and go back to Ruff and be a GOOD BOY, but the second little-dog voice inside my head—the naughty one—told me that if Duchess was here, having fun with all the other mutts, then I should keep having the time of my life. After all, if Stricker reported me to Hills Village Dog Shelter, we could report her dog, too...HA HA!

On I went...

178

Diving over ramps!

Jumping through hoops!

Bounding through tunnels!

Hurdling high bars!

Stumbling over seesaws!

It was wonderful!

But that's also when our humans caught up with us.

Before I had time to wriggle free, Ruff grabbed at my collar and clipped the leash to it.

"Junior?!" he panted. "What have you done? It's all ruin—"

Ruff didn't even have time to finish his sentence before Stricker burst into the agility ring and roared...

Ha ha! I've never seen a human look so angry. Stricker's whole body was shaking with rage. It looked like she might go off like a volcano in a cardigan!

"COME HERE NOW, DUCHESS, YOU ROTTEN MONGREL!"

What happened next is going to make you wet your pants with joy, my person-pal.

It turns out that Duchess was completely over being a polite pampered pedigree, and now she'd had a taste of freedom, there was no way she was turning back.

The judges who'd been watching our Basic Beginners course had now

made their way over and were all staring in disbelief at the canine carnage taking place.

"Duchess..." Stricker was now trying out a fake happy voice, but any dog with half a brain can sniff out one of those in a jiffy. "Duchy-Poo, come to Mommy."

Everybody held their breath to see what would happen next.

Don't forget that Iona Stricker and her now rebellious poodle—a rebel-oodle?—had been Best in Show winners for years.

Duchess the Wonder-Poo had NEVER misbehaved before.

"COME HERE!" Stricker screamed, losing her fake cool. "NOOOOOOOOW!"

"NOT ON YOUR LIFE, YOU BOSSY OLD CAT LOVER!" Duchess shouted at her human. Naturally, none of the people watching understood this, but all of us dogs did and it felt GREAT to hear.

With that, Duchess spun around in a full circle, then took a poop on the top end of the teeter-totter, while the audience gasped in dismay. HA HA!

And so . . . that was that . . . The fun had to end at some point, I guess.

After a few seconds the judges made up their minds and announced . . .

185

Well, you didn't think they were going to crown me champion after causing all that fuss, did you? Ha! Nope, I became a different sort of champion today.

SO...LET'S GET TO THE GRAND FINALE!

Once all the excitement had died down and most of the humans had taken their pooch-pals off for a spot of shopping, there was just me, Ruff, and Stricker left in the ring. (Duchess had run off to the food stalls to snatch up a few leftovers.)

"My aunt was right about you!" Stricker snapped at Ruff. I swear I could see smoke coming out of her nostrils. "You are just an uncouth, bad-mannered, unimpressive WASTE OF TIME!"

She was practically foaming at the mouth

as she slowly stalked toward us.

"You may have tempted my darling Duchy-Poo over to the naughty side of the fence, BUT YOU STILL DIDN'T WIN ANYTHING! YOU AND YOUR DOG ARE ZERO, LOSER NOBODIES!"

And that's when I spotted she had stepped on the lowered end of the closest seesaw. I looked up and searched for Odin in the crowd, but immediately saw he'd spotted it, too, and was charging toward us.

It happened in a strange kind of slow motion. Odin leaped into the air and I joined him. We came thumping down on the other end of the seesaw and...

Well, let's just say old Stricker is going to be smelling of Meaty-Giblet-Jumble-Chum for quite a while.

10:30 p.m.

Ah, my person-pal, you've reached the last teensy part of my story.

Wasn't it great?

Well, it's not over yet! There's one last detail I haven't told you...

It turns out that the Debonair Dandy-Dog Show has a special novelty prize each year for the worst-trained dog, and you are holding

189

the diary of that AWESOME, UNCONTROL-
LABLE POOCH in your hands.

I'm sitting here on the comfy squishy thing
in the Picture Box Room surrounded by a
year's supply of Meaty-Giblet-Jumble-Chum!!

Ha ha! RULES AREN'T FOR EVERYBODY!

Wait till you see what I'm up to next week!! Now, get out of here...I want to be alone with my feast!!

Happy pooching...
Junior x

How to speak Doglish
A human's essential guide to speaking paw-fect Doglish!

PEOPLE

Peoplish	Doglish
Owner	Pet human
Grandma	Grandmoo
Grandpa	Grand-paw
Mom	Mom-Lady
Georgia	Jawjaw
Rafe	Ruff
Khatchadorian	Catch-A-Doggy-Bone

PLACES

Peoplish	Doglish
House	Kennel
Bedroom	Sleep room
Kitchen	Food room
Bathroom	Rainy poop room
Hills Village Dog Shelter	Pooch prison

THINGS

Peoplish	Doglish
Shower	Drippy water box
Toilet	Emergency water bowl
Toilet paper	Toy paper
TV	Picture box
Sofa	Comfy squishy thing
Car	Moving people-box on wheels
Vacuum cleaner	Most evil creature in the world

READ ON FOR FUN ACTIVITIES!

Dot-To-Dot

Connect the dots from 1 to 85 to complete the picture!

WORD SEARCH

Can you spot some of Junior's doggy
friends in the word search?

Turn to the back to find out if you're right!

L	D	T	N	S	P	A	N	I	E	L	O	P
S	A	V	K	C	A	D	O	O	U	E	H	O
L	C	B	I	H	K	T	S	B	Y	O	G	O
T	H	Z	R	N	L	I	N	O	T	N	T	D
G	S	Q	P	A	Z	H	T	X	Q	B	E	L
B	H	M	C	U	D	U	I	E	S	E	D	E
U	U	J	K	Z	B	O	P	R	R	R	X	W
K	N	U	B	E	A	T	R	O	E	G	V	S
L	D	S	C	R	Q	P	X	L	U	E	B	A
C	H	I	H	U	A	H	U	A	J	R	N	T
A	R	T	Y	K	A	T	A	P	O	E	F	M
F	R	E	N	C	H	B	U	L	L	D	O	G

(LOLA)

(BETTY)

(GENGHIS)

(DIEGO)

LABRADOR • DACHSHUND • LEONBERGER
FRENCH BULLDOG • CHIHUAHUA • SCHNAUZER
POODLE • BOXER • SPANIEL

ANSWERS!

DOT-TO-DOT

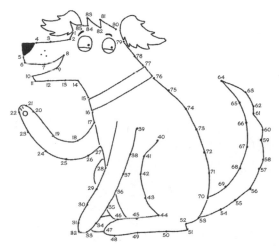

WORD SEARCH

L	D	T	N	S	P	A	N	I	E	L	O	P
S	A	V	K	C	A	D	O	O	U	E	H	O
L	C	B	I	H	K	T	S	B	Y	O	G	O
T	H	Z	R	N	L	I	N	O	T	N	T	D
G	S	Q	P	A	Z	H	T	X	Q	B	E	L
B	H	M	C	U	D	U	I	E	S	E	D	E
U	U	J	K	Z	B	O	P	R	R	R	X	W
K	N	U	B	E	A	T	R	O	E	G	V	S
L	D	S	C	R	Q	P	X	L	U	E	B	A
C	H	I	H	U	A	H	U	A	J	R	N	T
A	R	T	Y	K	A	T	A	P	O	E	F	M
F	R	E	N	C	H	B	U	L	L	D	O	G

A **MIDDLE SCHOOL** STORY

DOG DIARIES
Happy Howlidays!

CREATOR OF *MAX EINSTEIN*

JAMES PATTERSON

WITH STEVEN BUTLER

A MIDDLE SCHOOL STORY

DOG DIARIES

HAPPY HOWLIDAYS!

JAMES PATTERSON

WITH STEVEN BUTLER

ILLUSTRATED BY RICHARD WATSON

HELLO, MY FURLESS FRIEND!!

Oh boy, oh boy, OH BOY...you opened my new book!

I tell ya, I couldn't be more excited to know you're holding *HAPPY HOWLIDAYS!* in your five fingery digits, and we're about to go on a festive adventure together. Humans are my favorite...you're THE GREATEST, and I can feel a yip-yappy Happy Dance coming on.

This is a bark-tastic moment! It's WAGGY-TAIL-ICIOUS!! WHOA…hang on a second…I'm getting way ahead of myself.

What if you haven't read any of my PAW-SOME stories before?

Could that be possible?

Well, if you haven't, I'd say you're in desperate need of some serious poochification.

Now, I know what you're probably thinking. You'll be sitting there right now, scratching your head in that way that humans do even when they don't have fleas, wondering to yourself…*Poochification? What's that?*

Don't you worry, my person-pal, I'll explain all of it. Y'see, my book is practically a manual of muttness. It's a canine crash course! SLOBBER SCHOOL!

If you read this dog diary, you'll be living

206

a happier, bouncier, barking-at-raccoons-in-the-backyard-ier life in no time. I PROMISE!

But there are definitely a few things you should know before we dive in, snout-first.

First of all, I'M JUNIOR...HELLO!

Ha! I love saying that!

Dogs don't usually bother with hellos. We normally just take a quick sniff of each other's butts, but I learned early on that humans aren't so into that...HA HA!

The other thing I need to tell you about is...well...ummm...I didn't want to start things off like this, my furless friend, but there's no way around it. For me to begin this story properly...like PROPERLY-PROPERLY... you need to hear about what I've been up to, and it includes one of the ugliest words in the Doglish language...it's a HORRIBLE word...DISGUSTING!! Even the bravest of hounds have run howling for the hills at the sound of it!

Brace yourself, before you turn the page.

Steady those nerves.

Breathe in...breathe out...then hide yourself

in the laundry pile or under your bed.

Are you ready? Okay...

UGH! It's one of the worst words ever, and I heard it WAY TOO MANY TIMES this summer.

Yep...if you've not read Book One in my totally lick-a-rific series, you missed out on hearing all about how I had to endure the nightmarish...the no-tummy-rubs-or-treats-ish...PERFECT POOCH OBEDIENCE SCHOOL FOR DOGS.

It was awful, my person-pal! There were moments back in those classes at the Hills Village dog park when I felt sure I was a goner. I thought my brain was going to melt into a big blob of Meaty-Giblet-Jumble-Chum and ooze out of my ears, IT WAS SOOOOOO BORING!!

212

Imagine it! A poor pooch like me being stuck with Iona Stricker and her pampered poo- dle, having to roll over, sit down, and play dead, when I should have been chasing raccoons and sniffing around the jungle gym with my bestest mutt-mates.

"WHAT A WAY TO SPEND YOUR SUM- MER, JUNIOR!" I hear you say....

But don't you fret, my furless friend. You didn't think I gave in to old Stricty-Pants Stricker, did you?

NEVER!!

I sure showed her. I don't want to give too much away, but it was me who walked away from the annual DEBONAIR DANDY- DOG SHOW with a year's supply of dog food and not Stricker's prim and proper princess-poodle Duchess. But I'm not gonna tell you how...

Ha ha! I wish you could have been there, my friend, it was TERRIFIC! But I couldn't have done any of it without the help of my best-best-BESTEST pet human, Ruff Catch-A-Doggy-Bone.

Just look at that face. I swear, I adore all you BRILLIANT humans, but there's nobody in the whole world that makes me wag my tail and perform a Happy Dance like Ruff. He's the greatest pet a dog like me could wish for.

RAFE KHATCHADORIAN

Ruff Catch-A-Doggy-Bone

Anyway...where was I? Ah yes, I'd say that's about enough snuffling down memory lane for now. We're already on page twelve and there's SO much more I need to tell you about.

You see, crazy things have been happening around Hills Village. REALLY WEIRD THINGS!!

I mean it, my person-pal. You won't believe your ears when I tell you what's been going on.

Are you now ready to dive in, snout-first?

Okay...don't forget to bring some treats and maybe a chew toy in case you need a few breaks along the way. I promise to tell you all the good bits and I won't leave any of it out.

Here we go!!

Tuesday

Now, I don't know what you and your human families like to get up to in your home towns, but here in Hills Village things get real strange toward the end of the year when everything gets colder.

I'd heard about all this weird stuff before, but with all the chaos and business of obedience classes (YUCK!!) over the summer, it had completely slipped my mutt-mind.

It wasn't until a few days ago when I was

minding my own business, chewing a Twisty-Chum-Chomper-Stick that I'd hidden in the Picture Box Room, that I heard Mom-Lady talking to Grandmoo on the chatty-ear-stick...

We've got LOTS of planning to do. It's nearly the HOLIDAY SEASON!

The Howliday Season!

It couldn't be true, could it? The fabled human howlidays of myth and legend?!

Oooh, I should probably explain myself…

A quick history…

Let's go back to my days at the Hills Village Dog Shelter, or, as us mutts like to call it, "POOCH PRISON": Me and my four-legged friends were stuck in a cage right next to Old Mama Mange. She was very, very, very, very, very old and had been behind bars for as long as anyone could remember—practically a squillion centuries when you think about it in dog years.

Anyway…late at night, when the warden had nodded off in front of the picture box in his office, Old Mama Mange would hobble up to the bars and tell us the most amazing stories from her life before she ended up in the slobbering slammer...the canine clink!

All her stories were most excellent, but there was one she'd jabber on about more than any other...

None of us ever really believed her, but now there I was, overhearing my own Catch-A-Doggy-Bone pack talking about THE HOWLIDAY SEASON!

Have you ever heard of anything as exciting as a whole season for howling?!?! Well, I hadn't!

I could barely stop myself from leaping into a Happy Dance right there on the Picture Box Room rug!

If everything Old Mama Mange had said was completely true, the Howliday Season was the biggest and best of all the human howlidays, and that's saying something. The people of Hills Village LOVE 'EM! They have so many, it's hard to count on all four paws.

224

I'm not even joking, my furless friend! I got a good look at Mom-Lady's calendar on the Food Room wall once and it was practically stuffed with howlidays of all sorts.

Don't believe me? I'll tell you...

The year starts with NEW EARS DAY.

Then there's MARTIN LUTHER KING CHARLES CAVALIER'S BIRTHDAY. I'm not sure who he was, but he seems like one important spaniel.

There's GEORGE WASHY-TONGUE'S BIRTHDAY...the lickiest President there ever was.

In the summer there's INKY-PEN-DANCE DAY! This is a real big party. It's a special howliday for scribbling all over the walls, then celebrating with enormous flashy sky-bangers! Us pooches are terrified of them, but the humans of Hills Village can't get enough.

AND THEN...

TA-DAA! We get to the best of them all! THE HOWLIDAY SEASON!!

The biggest and most bark-tastic part of the year...

Old Mama Mange told us so many stories about Fangsgiving and Critter-Mess Day and it all sounds SO much fun. A howliday where you get brand-new teeth, followed by one filled with nothing but making a giant mess stuffing your face with delicious snacks like CANINE CRISPY CRACKERS?!?!

BLISS!!!

Wednesday

I can barely contain my excitement, my person-pal. It's all coming true!

Ever since I heard Mom-Lady mention the Howliday Season on the chatty-ear-stick, I've been keeping my pooch-peepers on high alert for clues.

And guess what? THERE ARE CLUES EVERYWHERE! Just look at the backyard! It's all changing and I can definitely tell that my first-ever winter outside of the Hills Village

Dog Shelter is on its way.

Come on, I'll show you...

This all HAS to be something to do with the Howliday Season, I'm sure of it!

Yellow leaves
Whole piles of leaves...
...great for jumping through and taking private poops!

It's all very paw-some! I have no idea why the trees have gone bald and left their leaves on the ground. Go figure! Maybe they're getting real old? Maybe they've just been careless, or maybe they left them as a gift to all the people and pooches out there?

I mean it!! I can't think of anything nicer!

If you've never kicked about through a pile of crisp leaves before, you are definitely in need of a little more poochification, my furless friend. It's one of my favorite poochish pastimes!

So far it's definitely been the best part of the howlidays...

Ooooooh, speaking of the best part of the howlidays...the next special event of the season is happening tomorrow, and I'm feeling giddy about this one!

With the backyard all crunch-ified and whispers of excitement in the air, I've been listening to every conversation that happens at mealtime and I'm taking note of anything that sounds remotely howliday-ish. I'm learning SO MUCH about all the strange things people like to celebrate at this time of year, and most of it is completely BONKERS!

This next special day is the first BIG ONE of the season.

YOU GUESSED IT...

FANGSGIVING!!

Everyone in the Catch-A-Doggy-Bone pack seems to be super excited about it... including me!

Imagine a special day all about giving other people a new set of chompers. I couldn't invent a more poochish celebration if I tried!

I personally couldn't be prouder that Ruff, Jawjaw, Mom-Lady, and even Grandmoo are finally going to get their properly proper canine teeth and become more poochish than ever! They'll be chomping their way through all sorts of things in no time! If they're lucky, I might even show them the best chair leg to chew on in the Food Room, or what kind of tasty stinky socks are easiest to shred, ha ha!

9 a.m.

Oh boy, oh boy, OH BOY! I can tell that Fangsgiving is going to be just TER-RIFIC! How could it not be?

Mom-Lady says we're going to feast on TURKEY tomorrow, and she needs to go and pick it up, ready for the family feast!

I definitely know what turkey is! There's no mystery there...no sirree. I know EXACTLY what it is. After all, I've tried it lots of times!

Turkeys are lumpy, squidgy, smooshy blob-creatures who are kinda pinky/grayish in color and they live in little metal Meaty-Giblet-Jumble-Chum cans.

Ha! Told you I knew!!

It's the strangest of animals to look at, all gloopy dollops. It doesn't do much, but it really, really loves sitting in food bowls and being eaten, which is very lucky because it's also DEEEEEEEELICIOUS!!

A TURKEY'S NATURAL HABITAT

9:28 a.m.

And we're off, my person-pal. Mom-Lady and I are in the moving people-box on wheels and we're heading to the turkey farm to pick up our very own EXTRA-LARGE turkey!

Whoever heard of a turkey farm?!? I've never seen one before, but I'm willing to bet it looks a lot like this...

11:33 a.m.

Errrm...

We've just arrived back at the kennel and Mom-Lady carried something huge out of the back of the moving people-box on wheels. I sat in the front seat the whole time but didn't see our extra-large turkey when she collected it at the farm store and put it in the trunk. Only, just now, I caught a glimpse of it as Mom-Lady went into the Food Room...and it's MASSIVE!!

Extra-large cans of food aren't usually *that* much bigger than the regular kind—this thing was the size of all Ruff's Sleep Room pillows piled together! It was inside a huge shopping bag, so I didn't get a good look, but OH BOY are we going to be feasting tomorrow!

12 p.m.

Aaaagh! This is so frustrating, my person-pal! All I want to do is get a peek at the enormous can of turkey, but Mom-Lady has banned me, Ruff, and Jawjaw from going into the Food Room. She says…

1 p.m.

Ruff and Jawjaw have been tasked with decorating the Picture Box Room, so I've tagged along to watch.

It's so funny to us dogs how humans hang stuff up on walls to celebrate an occasion. You can be super strange sometimes, HA HA! I just don't get what it's for...

I remember feeling SO confused back in the springtime when we had a party for

Grandmoo—because she'd turned another year older, I think. I just couldn't understand why Mom-Lady was so worried about hanging up long ropes of little flaggy things and blowing up colorful blobs filled with her breath, when there were far more important things to pay attention to…like the table FILLED with food or barking through the front door every time another guest arrived.

Anyway…Ruff is now hanging twisty loops of yellowy/leafy twigs on the wall, and Jawjaw has been arranging little round orange things on the window ledge. At first I thought they were balls for playing fetch with and snatched one when Jawjaw wasn't looking, but the whole thing turned out to be some sort of vegetable and went crunch in my mouth when I least expected it. Loads of stringy seeds and bits of squidgy goop exploded everywhere!

Why would humans want to decorate their kennels with exploding VEGETABLES???

NOTE TO SELF:

Keep away from the little orange decorations—they taste like poop and healthy stuff. BLEEEUUUGH!!!!

2:17 p.m.

There are wonderful, nose-tickling smells wafting down the hallway from the Food Room and I'm trying to do anything I can to not think about the giant can of dog food we're all going to be enjoying for Fangsgiving tomorrow. Be still, my houndy heart!!

3:21 p.m.

This is unbearable! Whatever Mom-Lady is cooking up on the other side of the Food Room door smells so delicious I've lost control of my paws. My feet keep hopping and twitching about with pure excitement!!

4:45 p.m.

I'm not going to make it to Fangsgiving at this rate, my furless friend. All the whiff-tastic smells are making my stomach growl louder than a bear with a bellyache!

4:57 p.m.

I…I…I can't concentrate…I can't relax…I can't stop myself from drooling at the thought of all that turkey…

Mom-Lady put my regular food bowl in the hall while she's cooking, but I can't even look at my normal food anymore. It's just so UN-TURKEY-ISH! I'm going to drool myself to death…

5:04 p.m.

Any minute now...I...I...I can feel my life slipping away...*cough*...GOODBYE, CRUEL WORLD! I can't go on a minute longer without that turkey tastiness...*splutter*...just need a...*whimper*...turkey treat...or...seven...

5:12 p.m.

DEAD!

5:36 p.m.

STILL DEAD!

5:46 p.m.

EVEN MORE DEAD!

5:51 p.m.

SO DEAD,
COULDN'T
GET ANY
DEADER!!

6 p.m.

Okay, okay, okay...I'm not dead! I may have overreacted a little, but that was a close one, I'm telling ya!

I finally managed to distract myself from all the yumma-lumptious smells by sneaking into Jawjaw's room and stealing one of the creepy little plastic humans she keeps on the shelf above her bed.

Hey! Don't judge me, all right? These are desperate times, and only one of the *forbidden* chew toys was enough to take my mind off things. Who could blame me at a time like this, anyway?

I'm never supposed to go in Jawjaw's Sleep Room. She gets super grumpalicious if I ever sneak inside. Yep! It's strictly out of bounds...so, of course, the things inside her room taste far more interesting than any-thing else around the kennel.

I've stashed it in Ruff's laundry pile for now, though. He's been calling me from the Picture Box Room and I don't want to be found out. I'll go see what he wants...

7:33 p.m.

Check, check… This is roving reporter Junior Catch-A-Doggy-Bone, coming to you live from the comfy squishy thing.

BREAKING NEWS

Ha ha! Just joking with you! I've always wanted to say that after seeing it on the picture box.

But...guess what? Ruff and I snuggled in to watch a TV show all about Fangsgiving and I'm learning heaps about it. I mean...my understanding of the Peoplish language is a little crummy, but I think I've got the basics of the Fangsgiving story. Wanna hear?

Okay...settle down, get all comfy and listen to this...

THE STORY OF FANGSGIVING

Long, long ago, when the world was practically a puppy and Meaty-Giblet-Jumble-Chum hadn't even been invented yet, a pack of Pilgrim Pooches and their pet humans swam all the way to Hills Village from the other side of the planet. **WHOOO-WEEEE,** that's a long way!

They bravely traveled into the unknown, looking for a life filled with mountains of treats, super-tickly tummy-rubs, and a comfortable place to poop, but when they arrived, they discovered a pack of majestic native Hills Village-ians instead.

At first, the Hills Village-ians and their hunting hounds were very wary of the Pilgrim Pooches and their pet humans, but before long they all got together for a doggy-licious dinner party—they ate a lot, danced a lot, and ever since then, on the fourth Thursday of November, families get together to celebrate and give fangs to those who need 'em. That explains the name of the howliday!

THE END

There! I definitely missed a few facts along the way, but I'm pretty sure I got most of the story right. It all makes so much more sense now…sort of…

10:30 p.m.

I can't sleep, my furless friend. Everyone headed off to their Sleep Rooms early, ready for a big day of celebrating tomorrow, but I just can't get the thought of all that marvelous meat out of my brain.

I've tried everything I can, but nothing works! Putting my head under Ruff's pillow. Lying on my back with my paws in the air.

Counting sheep in my head. That last one is something Old Mama Mange told me to try when we were having a bad night back in pooch prison. But before I'd even realized it, the sheep had transformed themselves into cans of delicious turkey and were taunting me with their tastiness.

11:08 p.m.

There's nothing for it, my person-pal. If I stand any chance of getting to sleep tonight, I'm going to have to go and take just the tiniest of peeks at what Mom-Lady has prepared in the Food Room.

Now, I know what you're thinking. You're reading this and saying, "No! Junior, you're going to get into so much trouble! You'll never be able to resist all that tummy-tingling food!" and you'd be right...normally.

But...I have a cunning plan. Just to make sure I'm not tempted to snack on anything and get myself into hot water, I'm bringing along Jawjaw's creepy little plastic human I stashed in the laundry pile earlier. That way, if I have any sudden urges to gobble up what Mom-Lady's cooked, I can chew on the plastic toy instead. IT'S FOOLPROOF!

11:45 p.m.

Psssst! Are you there? Oh good...it's so dark in the hallway.

Okay, I'm just going to sneak into the Food Room, take a quick look around, and I'll be out of there and back on the bed in a jiffy. No harm done, right?

Here I go...

Midnight

HOLD EVERYTHING!!! I know it's late, my furless friend, but I've just gotta tell you about what I saw. You wouldn't believe your person-peepers.

I nudged the Food Room door open and was instantly hit by a dizzying mix of fantastic aromas and delicious whiffs. One of the little lights above the counter had been left on, so I got a good view of everything, and…

well…I'm not afraid to admit it brought a tear to this mutt's eye.

The table had been decorated with fancy cloths and decked out with flowers and candles and more of those little exploding orange vegetables. Mom-Lady had been baking all day and there were biscuits and rolls piled up under a glass dome.

The kitchen counter was lined with bowls and dishes of tasty-smelling foods and sauces, waiting to be cooked and feasted upon for tomorrow's Fangsgiving dinner, and…

I looked up…

I looked down…

I sniffed in every corner of the room…

Where was the enormous can of turkey? It had to be here someplace.

I snuffled about the room for a few minutes, trying to figure out where it could be. The turkey can wasn't on the table, and it wasn't lined up on the counter ready to be cooked.

Just then a thought flashed across my barky-brain and I gasped. There was only one place Mom-Lady kept the meaty food before she cooked it in the hot fire box for dinner…

I put Jawjaw's creepy plastic human on the
floor, then grabbed one of the stinky wash
cloths from its hook. Swinging my head
from side to side, I managed to
loop it through the coldy frosty
tall thing's handle. Then I pulled
with all my mutt-might.

At first the door didn't want to budge. I struggled and tugged but nothing moved.

I couldn't give up now! There was no way I was going to leave the Food Room without seeing the turkey for myself. With thoughts of the giant can of meat skipping across my mind, I gave it one last enormous yank and the coldy frosty tall thing burst open in a cloud of chilly fog.

For a second, the bright light from inside the tall box blinded me and I squinted my eyes against it. My fur prickled with a mixture of excitement and the icy air that swirled around my paws.

This was it: I was going to see the...

AAAAAAAAAGH!!

Suddenly my houndy heart leaped up into my throat as I saw what was sitting in the fridge.

There must be some mistake. Had Mom-Lady gone absolutely crazy?!

Instead of a neat tin can filled with squidgy blobby globs of turkey, she'd brought home some kind of giant headless BALDY BIRD!!

I scampered across the floor and darted under the table, expecting the ugly creature to attack at any moment.

Safely tucked behind the tablecloth, I tried to stop myself from panting with surprise and listened as hard as I could for signs that the great big baldy beast was preparing to pounce.

I waited…
I waited…
I waited…
Nothing.

Sniffing the air, I peeked out from under the cloth and stared at the weird animal sitting in the open coldy frosty tall thing. I gave it a few test growls and even tried darting toward it and then running away very fast to see what it did.

The baldy bird didn't move.

I sniffed the air again and caught the scent of salty, fatty deliciousness. It was even better than the pong of Meaty-Giblet-Jumble-Chum!

Maybe this beast in the cold box wasn't a dog-eating terror from the land of nightmares.

I crept back toward it, preparing to dart away at a second's notice, but still the creature didn't move.

It just sat there like Lola after she's gobbled down a full bowl of Doggo-Drops.

Now I was close, I could see it was sitting in a big tray filled with sliced vegetables and green leafy stuff. Mom-Lady had covered it in zingy-smelling oil and sprinkled salt and pepper all over it. WOWZERS! This was one pampered partridge...a glamorous

goose...A LUXURIOUS
LUNCH!! Ha ha!

There was an open-
ing in the baldy bird
(I think it was its mouth), and
Mom-Lady had put lots of sliced lemons
and tufts of green stuff in there. I guess the
strange thing must have been hungry.

Just then I couldn't help but feel a little
sorry for the salty and peppery baldy bird.
It certainly wasn't going to be able to join in
the fun of Fangsgiving after it went to cook
in the hot fire box tomorrow morning, so I
decided to give it a gift, just from me. It is
the Howliday Season, after all...

I grabbed Jawjaw's creepy little human
and placed it in with the sliced lemons and
tufty leaves. That way the baldy bird could

have one last night of waggy-tail-icious snacking on one of the tastiest forbidden chew toys in the whole kennel. It was the least I could do...

12:24 a.m.

My work here is done, my person-pal. I've seen the festive baldy bird...I've spread a little howliday cheer...and I can feel a long, happy nap coming on.

See you tomorrow!

Thursday

6 a.m.

Wake up! Wake up! WAKE UP! Good morning, my furless friend. It's finally here!! Fangsgiving has arrived and I can't wait to celebrate with my new set of gnawy-gnashing fangs. I might try chewing through the tree in the backyard this afternoon! That'll surprise the raccoons!! Ha ha!

I'm just going to race about the kennel and wake everyone up the way they enjoy the most...with a good paw-poke right in the center of their forehead. Won't be a sec...

10 a.m.

No one has handed out the new teeth yet but Grandmoo's come over with cookies of the human and canine variety, and we're watching a huge parade on the picture box.

I swear I've never seen anything like it, but I couldn't be a happier hound...well...not until the feast. Ha! I can't wait to try great big baldy bird for the first time!!

2 p.m.

It's time!! We've all been summoned into the Food Room and we're preparing to sit down and feast together as the Catch-A-Doggy-Bone pack. Mom-Lady is even going to let me sit at the table with my own dog bowl filled with delicious dog-elicacies.

2:12 p.m.

Oh, you should see it, my person-pal! The table is all set...I'm not sure what all the foods are, but I listened real hard to Grand-moo, and as far as I can tell there's...

~~SWEET POTATOES~~
Swonk potatoes

~~BUTTERNUT~~
~~SQUASH~~
~~SOUP~~
Bumble-butt
squashed soup

~~STUFFING~~
Stuff

~~GRAVY~~
Groovy sauce

~~GREEN BEANS~~
Grim bean

~~CRANBERRY SAUCE~~
Crumb-bungle sauce

~~PECAN PIE~~
Peeking
Pie

You name it, Mom Lady has cooked it!
The only thing we're waiting for now is the grand finale!! The great big roasted baldy bird! It's going to be SPECTACULAR!!

2:16 p.m.

UH-OH! NO, NO, NO, NO, NO!!!
Mom-Lady has just pulled the bird from the hot fire box and already I can smell that something isn't right. My nose is super, super, super stronger than my pet humans' and I don't think they've noticed it yet, but I definitely smell a plastic-ish, funky stink coming from the roast. Something tells me I maybe shouldn't have put Jawjaw's creepy

little human inside the baldy bird before it was cooked.

I'll just keep quiet and hope no one notices…

4 p.m.

So much for no one noticing, my furless friend!!

One minute it was "HAPPY FANGSGIV-ING!" and the next it was…

I RUINED FANGSGIVING!!!!!!!

5:26 p.m.

Oh, it's awful, my person-pal. I've never felt so rotten in my mutt-life.

Mom-Lady was furious when she found the melted creepy plastic human inside the turkey. I thought she was going to breathe flames and explode like one of the little orange vegetables!

To make matters worse, Mom-Lady blamed Jawjaw and sent her straight to her Sleep Room without any Fangsgiving snacks at all. I tried to explain that it was all my fault, I really did, but my pet humans are crummy at understanding Doglish and they just stared at me like I'd gone loop-the-loop Crazy with a capital C!!

I never intended to spoil the Fangsgiving feast and, even though I'm not one of Jawjaw's biggest fans, I didn't want to get her into trouble.

7:14 p.m.

Okay, my furless friend. I'm keeping a seriously low profile behind the comfy squishy thing in the Picture Box Room.

Mom-Lady ended up having to call in pizza, which put her in an even moodier mood after all the care she'd taken with the big baldy bird.

But…it's not all bad…I guess… Ruff managed to convince his mom to order a triple chunky cheese and hot dog pizza with extra-crunchy crusts. OUR FAVORITE!!

Grandmoo complained all evening…

...and Mom-Lady refused to eat a single slice out of sheer grumpaliciousness, but Ruff and I actually had a pretty GREAT Fangsgiving feast all to ourselves.

I suppose you could almost say that by breaking the rules and sneaking into the Food Room when I wasn't supposed to...and putting the creepy little human (which I wasn't supposed to have) into the big baldy bird... and accidentally making the whole meal taste like burnt plastic...I actually improved the howliday, right?

OF COURSE I'M RIGHT!

Without my expert help, there would NEVER have been triple chunky cheese and hot dog pizza with extra-crunchy crusts at the Fangsgiving table...and everything's better with pizza. Ha ha!

Yep—after careful consideration, I'm pretty sure I actually saved the day.

I'm going to sleep well tonight, my person-pal. I just wish I could figure out when they're going to hand out the brand-new sets of fangs...

Saturday

10:20 a.m.

Hmmmm...I may have been a little wrong about saving Fangsgiving, my person-pal.

I mean...I definitely think I definitely saved it definitely...but Mom-Lady is still super mad about the feast being ruined and I'm pretty certain Jawjaw is on to me. In fact, I know she is!

She keeps scowling every time she sees me...and...well...I wouldn't really mind—after all, Jawjaw used to scowl at me long before I spoiled the big baldy bird—but now she keeps muttering two words under her breath and they're the worst thing a mutt like me could ever want to hear. Especially from someone in his own pack.

It's true. Every time Jawjaw spots me in the Picture Box Room or she walks past Ruff's Sleep Room door and sees me curled up on the bed, she scrunches up her face and hisses...

Oh! They're the ugliest, scariest, most hateful words. My spine judders and I get a sickly swooshy feeling in my belly whenever someone says them out loud. It's left me feeling even guiltier than the time I buried Jawjaw's science project in the backyard and she got an F in class. That was a tail-between-my-legs kind of day, it really was, but this feels far worse...

Don't get me wrong—it's not the words Jawjaw said that are so horrible. It's what they mean and what they can lead to that scares us mutts. "Bad dog!" means no snacks. It means no tummy-rubs, or playing fetch in the dog park, or snuggles at bedtime, and... and...it can even mean a one-way ticket straight back to POOCH PRISON.

Ugh! I can hardly bring myself to say it!

I can't bear to think about Jawjaw seeing me as a B...a BA...a BAD...Oh, you know what I'm trying to say.

But triple chunky cheese and hot dog pizza with extra-crunchy crusts or no triple chunky cheese and hot dog pizza with extra-crunchy crusts, I can't let anything else go wrong this Howliday Season.

I've been hiding in the Rainy Poop Room a lot over the past few days and I've come up with a foolproof plan to make sure the Catch-A-Doggy-Bone pack have the best Critter-Mess Day EVER. I've decided that...

11 a.m.

Phew! I feel much better, my furless friend. If I make sure to keep that in mind from here on out, I know I can save the festivities and make this a Howliday Season to remember. That way, no one will ever think I'm a BAD DOG again.

1:21 p.m.

Ooooh! Ooooh! Ooooh! That's enough worrying for now, my person-pal. You won't believe what I've just seen.

Mom-Lady needed to go to the grocery store across town and she said I could go too for a walk. YIP-YIP-YIPPEE!!

Now, I always love taking Mom-Lady for a walk. It's not as much fun as going with Ruff, obviously, but it definitely has its perks.

If I wait patiently outside and don't bark at the other shoppers as they rattle about with those strange shopping cages on wheels, she buys some slices of chicken from the deli counter and gives me a piece.

And that's not even the best part!

Mom-Lady really likes exercise and always takes the long route home, which means…

DOGGY DRUMROLL, PLEASE!...we come back home via the Dandy Dog store!! It's one of my favorite places to visit in all of Hills Village, and I know that if I'm super good and I don't tug on the leash too much when we're walking, we can go in and have a good snuffle around.

I wish you could experience it, my person-pal. Behind that big green door is a pooch paradise, the likes of which you've never seen before. It's a dreamland for dogs! HOUND HEAVEN!!

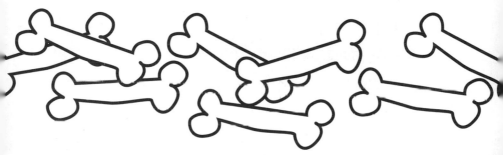

I get so excited when we go inside, I can't help but jump and yip about like a pup in a playground. It's a little undignified, but there's nothing I can do. You'd feel the same if you saw it, my furless friend, I just know you would. The Dandy Dog store is an entire shop filled with treats and snacks and toys and blankets and beds and balls and everything a dog could ever wish for.

But...it gets even better! You see, the best part of my walk with Mom-Lady wasn't just going inside my favorite shop, it was what I saw inside that wonderful place. Because today, on top of all the usual fantastic things to see and sniff and play with, the Dandy Dog store had been completely decorated!

My doggy eyes nearly rocketed out of my head with surprise. Everywhere I turned, there were twinkling lights and festive-looking red-and-white sticks hanging from the shelves. Jingly music was playing loudly and the shopkeeper was wearing a funny costume with pointy ears attached to his hat!

It was the most festiverous sight I'd ever laid my pooch-peepers on, I tell ya!

Mom-Lady gasped just as much as I did when she saw all the incredible decorations and hurried inside with me to have a look around.

I only had time to sniff the pile of braided rope toys before I spotted my pooch-pals Odin and Diego at the back of the store with their pet human and...

HA HA! Their pet had dressed them up in silly costumes just like the shopkeeper! Odin was wearing a knitted sweater with huge sprigs of holly on both sides, and Diego had on a little hat with a bell hanging off the end and little chihuahua-sized curly boots. It was HILARIOUS!

Even if nothing else happens for the rest of the year, seeing my pooch-pals all dressed up like that has to make this the BEST Howli-day Season EVER!! HA HA!

2:17 p.m.

Oh no, my person-pal, I spoke too soon!! This is terrible!!

It turns out while I was distracted and laughing at my mutt-mates and their dreadful Critter-Mess clothing, Mom-Lady had the same idea as their pet humans and was grabbing me a few outfits from the rack to try on.

AAAAAAAAAAGG-GGHHHH!!!

No, Junior! You vowed to be a good boy and nothing but a GOOD BOY!

Brace yourself, my furless friend. Looks like we're going clothes shopping...

2:23 p.m.

JUST LOOK AT ME!!!!

Well, that was humiliating! Honestly, if we weren't such good friends I'd be totally embarrassed about you just seeing that. I'll tell you what—if you keep my terrible festive fashion a secret, I'll share with you the Denta-Toothy-Chew I've got buried in one of Ruff's sneakers.

Deal?

Ha ha! Excellent!!

2:46 p.m.

Mom-Lady and I are nearly back at the Catch-A-Doggy-Bone kennel, and you wouldn't believe the crazy stuff I've just seen happening on my street.

After all the howllabaloo inside the Dandy Dog store, I certainly wasn't expecting any more surprises this afternoon, but it looks like the whole of Hills Village is preparing for the upcoming HO-HO-HO-est of howlidays. It's beginning to look a lot like Critter-Mess, that's for sure, my person-pal.

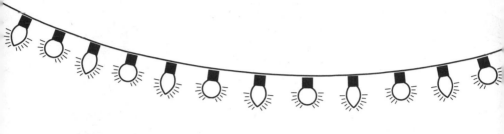

Mr. and Mrs. Haggerty, who live across the street from us, were out front, decking their house with strings of colored lights…

And the Hanleys were putting out models of strange animals with knobbly horns in the front yard. They were positioned like they were about to take off into the sky, pulling a great big red guy in a roofless moving people-box behind them.

I've heard about him before, my person-pal. The happy-looking red guy, I mean. Old Mama Mange talked about him once, back in my days at Hills Village Dog Shelter. If my memory serves me correctly, his name is Saint Lick and he lives up a pole someplace.

323

NOTE TO SELF:

Find out more about this Saint Lick character. I can't quite remember what Old Mama Mange had to say about him, but I have a feeling he's pretty important if you want to have a super-great Critter-Mess Day.

9:32 p.m.

What did I tell you, my furless friend? I knew Saint Lick was one to watch out for!

After dinner...Mom-Lady, Ruff, and Jawjaw had boring vegetables on spag-et-ig-a-li... spat-giggly...spa-tig-a-ti...I CAN'T SAY IT!! ...and I had a huge bowl of DOGGO-DROPS. They're one of my favorite types of mutt-meals!

Anyway! After chomping down as much as we could eat, Ruff and I went off to the Picture Box Room to watch some festivish films. We snuggled right in and watched one of those cartoony things called *The Night Before Critter-Mess*, and OH BOY did I learn a lot.

It turns out that on Critter-Mess Eve, Saint Lick travels all over the world...ALL OVER THE WORLD?? That means all the places that aren't in Hills Village. I didn't even know such places existed! And he goes to every kennel in every town and leaves presents in every room for the different family-packs to find

when they wake up on Critter-Mess Day...
AND if you're bad he leaves you a lump of
coal. I have no idea what that is, but doesn't
it sound wonderful?

I also learned that he only leaves the best
chew toys for the GOOD BOYS and GOOD
GIRLS. Well, that's that, my person-pal. I
definitely need to stick to my vow and be the
best-behaved pooch between now and the
big day.

Sunday

11:16 a.m.

Hold on a second, my furless friend! Something exciting is happening, I can tell. I stayed awake far too late last night, thinking about Saint Lick and all the amazing dog toys he's going to bring me, so I slept in a little late. But the moment I opened one eye and took my first sniff of the morning, I could sense that festive things were afoot... or *apaw*...Ha ha!

11:18 a.m.

This is AMAZING! I've just walked out of our Sleep Room to find Jawjaw and Mom-Lady pulling out a load of boxes from the hallway closet, and they're each filled with...with... decorations!!!

12 p.m.

I can barely stop myself from peeing right here on the carpet, my person-pal. Jawjaw and Ruff have been put in charge of untangling the long strings of twinkle-lights and Mom-Lady has just driven off in the moving people-box, saying she has a surprise for us...

12:11 p.m.

I'm being the most perfect pooch I know how to be and I'm waiting for Mom-Lady by the front door. That's what all GOOD BOYS do...

Ruff and Jawjaw are still grumbling down the hall, figuring out the lighty stringy things, but all I can think about is what Mom-Lady has gone to fetch. Maybe it's another BIG BALDY BIRD?

I'll wait right here and find out...

12:23 p.m.

Still waiting…

12:40 p.m.

STILL WAITING!!!

12:52 p.m.

Still wai—WAIT A SECOND! Did I just hear the moving people-box pull up outside?

Hold breath…

Hold breath…

Hold breath…

I did!!! OH BOY, OH BOY, OH BOY!! I can hear Mom-Lady's footsteps and the sound of something swooshy being dragged along the path to the front door. Any moment now she's going to walk inside, see me being the goodest GOOD BOY she's ever seen and give me the giftiest, surprisiest present I've ever—

1:30 p.m.

I...I...don't know what just happened, my furless friend. I was so terrified, I thought my hound-heart was going to play a tune on the inside of my ribs.

I'm safe here, under Ruff's bed, but out there in the hallway...I...I...I just saw a monster that made the horrifying vacuum cleaner seem nicer than a tummy-rub.

I'll explain...

There I was, waiting for Mom-Lady to bring home the surprise she'd promised, when... her keys jangled as she took them from her pocket...the key turned in the lock...and... and...A GREEN SPIKY MONSTER BURST THROUGH THE DOOR AND LURCHED TOWARD ME!

If I hadn't used my super-speedy dog powers and run away quicker than you can shout "RUN! IT'S A FESTIVE FIEND!" I swear, I would have been lunch.

1:36 p.m.

I can hear Mom-Lady and Ruff laughing in the hallway. Why aren't they screaming and darting for cover?

1:38 p.m.

Hmmmm…something's not quite right here. They've started playing Critter-Mess music from the musicy soundy box. As head pooch of the kennel, I think I need to go investigate. I'll keep you posted…

3 p.m.

IT WAS A TREE!?! Can you imagine it, my person-pal? I sneaked down the hallway, peeked around the Picture Box Room door, and there it was. Mom-Lady had stood it up over near the corner and Jawjaw and Ruff were starting to wrap the strings of twinkle-lights around it.

Just when I think I've got you humans all figured out, you go and do the strangest of things! Whoever heard of having a tree inside your kennel? They're supposed to be outside in the backyard so you can pee on them and bark at RACCOONS in the branches.

3:19 p.m.

Okay, I admit it—this is kinda fun. The Critter-Mess tree is now covered in little lights and I'm helping Ruff with the decorations. Every time he hangs one of the glittery balls on a low branch, I take it off again and bury it down the side of the comfy squishy thing.

Humans love it when dogs help out...I can tell...and the tree is looking paw-some! I still have no idea what it's doing inside the kennel, but it's certainly getting me in the mood for festive Critter-Mess cheer. HA HA!

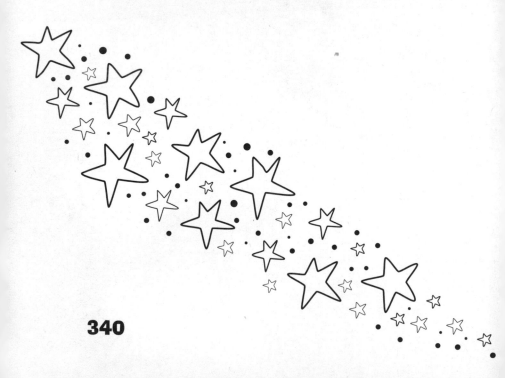

9 p.m.

I don't think I've ever been more content, my furless friend. Tonight, Mom-Lady baked cookies for Ruff and Jawjaw, and had bought an extra-big bag of Crunchy-Lumps for me, then we all sat watching a movie about a grumpy old man with a funny voice who didn't like Critter-Mess. In it, he was visited by three gusts. I don't really know what a gust is...or what was happening...but it was super WAGGY-TAIL-ICIOUS to curl up with my Catch-A-Doggy-Bone pack in a proper cuddle-puddle.

It might be my first-ever Howliday Season, but it's shaping up to be a great one. Sigh...

Monday

7 a.m.

Hold everything, my person-pal!
I…I…I don't know how many more shocks I can take! This Critter-Mess malarkey is so full of unexpected surprises.

Last night, after the movie, before I curled up on the end of Ruff's bed and went to sleep, things were completely normal. Well… as normal as they can ever be in the Catch-A-Doggy-Bone kennel.

But now…now everything's…everything's …vanished! The whole world outside! IT'S GONE!!!

I know I sound like I've had my doggy brains scrambled, or I've eaten too many Canine Crispy Crackers before dozing off and now I'm having a nightmare, but I swear I'm awake and I'm absolutely telling the truth. POOCH PROMISE!!

Let me explain…

Yesterday evening, right before heading off to bed, I went outside for a quick pee, poop, and a bark at our neighbor's cat who was trespassing on our fence.

Anyway…apart from the weird stuff I mentioned earlier, like all the leaves turning orange and then the trees going bald, everything in the backyard was pretty much the same as it always was.

But...

Me and Ruff got up this morning and headed to the Food Room for some hap-hap-happy breakfastin'—and that's when I spotted it! Outside the window, the whole world has turned WHITE!

Whiter than white! It's like some snatch-some sneak has made off with Hills Village while everybody was asleep.

THIS IS WHAT

IT LOOKED LIKE!

8 a.m.

I just don't understand my pet humans sometimes, my furless friend. Mom-Lady and Jawjaw are awake now too, and both of them
seem SO excited that the world is missing. I
swear, if either of them grew a tail, they'd be
wagging it like crazy and swatting furniture
halfway across the room, they're so happy.

Well, duh! How is anyone going to go to school when it's been erased? THERE IS NO SCHOOL!!

Sometimes I worry that I'm the only smart creature in the whole of the Catch-A-Doggy-Bone kennel. Honestly!

The problem is, Ruff is acting just as strangely. He threw open the curtains in the Picture Box Room and…where the street used to be…there was nothing…NOTHING!

"Great!" Ruff yelled.

Great? I looked at my pet human like he was bananas but he was too busy racing over to the other windows to notice me.

"I've never seen it like this so early in December," Mom-Lady joined in. "It's beautiful!"

BEAUTIFUL? THE WORLD IS MISSING!

"NO SCHOOL!" Jawjaw yelled as she

ran into the room. She was holding her little talky box in her hand. "I just checked. They said it's going to be closed all week by the looks of things!"

I could feel my heart starting to race. I know I overreacted about the Critter-Mess tree and the BIG BALDY BIRD on the night before Fangsgiving, but this one was a real mystery to me. How could there be anything great or beautiful about waking up to find the whole world has vanished?

8:54 a.m.

Ruff and Jawjaw are putting their coats and boots on. Are they...ARE THEY GOING OUTSIDE?!?!

9:03 a.m.

AAAGH! Goodbye, my furless friend. I can't believe I'm having to tell you this but...but...Ruff put the stupid hat that Mom-Lady bought me on my head, and now he's clipped the leash to my collar and is trying to pull me to the front door.

WHY?!? Why would my pet human want to drag his best-best-BESTEST GOOD BOY friend into the great white nothing? There's no way we'll make it out there in oblivion.

GOODBYE,
CRUEL WORLD!!!

9:06 a.m.

I…ummm…okay, Junior, just breathe…It's cold…the front path is cold and fluffy. If I can feel the ground is cold and fluffy, I'm definitely not dead! The air is full of tiny white things and…oh…they're landing on my nose…My paws are leaving prints where I walk…Ruff is calling my name and he's smiling…I think…I think this might be…

AMAZING!

9:10 a.m.

I don't know what all this white stuff is, my person-pal, but I think it might be the most exciting, paw-rific, amazerous, waggy-tail-icious thing I've ever experienced in my whole licky life!!

NOTE TO SELF:

At Critter-Mess time, when something seems scary and completely Crazy with a capital C, it's probably going to end up being completely terrific!

9:34 a.m.

I don't think this morning could get any better! Practically the whole neighborhood is out in the street and we're all having one giant CANINE CARNIVAL in the cold fluffy stuff.

My bestest pooch-pals are all here. I'll introduce you properly...

ODIN

Betty

LOLA

DIEGO

GENGHIS

Ha ha! It looks like all our pet humans have been to the Dandy Dog store to buy us some festive fashion! Suddenly my hat doesn't seem so bad…

3 p.m.

What a day it's been, my person-pal. I don't think I've had that much fun since I saw a raccoon and chased it up Mom-Lady's clean washing hanging on the line in the backyard. That was a good day…a terrific one…but this was even better!

Our humans all went off to the end of the street to throw balls of snow at each other— oh, that's what it's called, by the way: SNOW! I heard Lola's human talking about it, and you know how good I'm getting at understanding the Peoplish language.

Anyway...while they all went off for a snowball fight, me and my pooch-pals had a BARK-TASTIC day, getting up to all sorts of canine capers.

We rolled and scrambled and threw ourselves about in the stuff like we were puppies again.

Genghis and Lola showed off their artistic side...

...we each tried our hand at making our first-ever snowdogs...

...and Betty kept us entertained with more of her HOWL-ARIOUS jokes.

Ahhh, it was so great!

The Following Monday

10:22 a.m.

HELLO!!! Oh, I've missed you, my person-pal. I can't believe it's been a whole week! I wanted to write in my dog diary, I really did, but I've been so super busy, you wouldn't believe it!

Since we last talked, the snow hasn't stopped falling! It turns out this is the biggest

BLIZZARD (that's a new word I learned a few days ago) that Hills Village has EVER seen. We had so much snow last night, Mom-Lady and Ruff had to dig their way out of our front door. It was INCREDIBLE!

All you could see from the Picture Box Room window was their heads, bobbing around above the snow line.

Hills Village Middle School has been closed the whole time and looks like it'll stay that way until long after Critter-Mess Day, so I'm as pleased as a Labrador with a bowlful of leftovers. It means I've spent every day with Ruff and we've been out having the greatest adventures a mutt and his pet human could ask for.

Let me see, I'll fill you in on the best bits. There was sledding on the hill behind the grocery store…

…ice skating at the local rinkly-runk (whatever *that* is)…

…and I even got the chance to sneak off to the house of Stricty-Pants STRICKER and her pampered poodle Duchess and leave a few yellow patches in the snow on their front lawn, if you know what I mean? HA HA!!

It's been terrific! But the fun hasn't ended there, my furless friend. No sirree!

Tonight we're all off for some carol singing. I've got to admit, I have no idea who Carol is or why we're singing to her, but I think it's going to be a humdinger of a night.

I overheard Mom-Lady singing while she was in the Rainy Poop Room and I've memorized the words perfectly…

Jingle bells, Grandmoo smells

Of perfume and of tea.

Old Saint Lick got such a shock,

Climbing down the chimney!

OH!!!!!

Jingle bells, Jawjaw smells,

So Saint Lick ran away...

Now she won't get any gifts

To open Critter-Mess Day!!

I don't know if I've told you before, my person-pal, but I have a BRILLIANT singing voice. It's true. I'm going to be the best GOOD BOY of them all tonight. Just you wait and see...

8:30 p.m.

What did I tell you?!? NAILED IT!!

Thursday

Well, whadda-ya-know!? I learned a whole heap of new stuff at the dog park today, my furless friend. It turns out that not all humans celebrate the Howliday Season with Fangsgiving and Critter-Mess Day.

Betty's pet human celebrates another holiday...she called it HANUUUUUUKKAH!

And Lola's pet celebrates another one altogether! They call it KWANZAA!

I don't know much about Kwanzaa, but Lola says they have lots of food, too, so it sounds pretty BARK-A-LICIOUS if you ask me.

Friday

Today I found the BEST chew toys hanging under the window ledge outside the Food Room when I was out in the backyard. They're coldy, crunchy, pointy things and they are ACE for biting on. I've called them ACE-ICLES!!

Saturday

2 p.m.

Today, Mom-Lady, Ruff, and Jawjaw have all gone off to the mall to do some shopping for gifts, so I'm over at Genghis's kennel with Lola and Betty. It's so weird, my person-pal. I had no idea that one home could be so different from another.

Genghis's kennel is nothing like our

Catch-A-Doggy-Bone one. It's huge and everything smells like lemon dish soap. His pet human is super funny as well.

Wherever we go in the house, Genghis's pet follows us with a broom and handfuls of dusters and cleaning spray, like the stuff Mom-Lady keeps under the sink. It's like he actually enjoys cleaning!

Whoever heard of anybody who likes tidying up? MAKING A MESS IS THE FUN PART!!

2:37 p.m.

Oh no, my person-pal! Just when I thought there weren't going to be any more scares before Critter-Mess Day, I've just overheard something that has made the hairs on the back of my neck stand on end. Something so terrible, I think I might need to have a lie down.

I can tell you what I've just discovered, but you've got to promise me you're feeling in a brave mood!

Do not turn to the next page if you're squeamish, nervous, or inclined to pee your human pants with fear!

Well done, my furless friend. You're clearly very brave.

Okay, so I'm going to tell you what I just heard. Brace yourself!

Genghis's owner finally got tired of tidying up after us dogs and took us all out to the back-yard. We were all there, doing our business, if you know what I mean. The pet human got a poop bag ready in his hands and then he said…

At first I didn't think anything of it, until
I realized the crazy guy was talking about
poops...POOPS!! That's what the word "presents" means!!!

383

My head started racing and my memory flashed back to the night I watched *The Night Before Critter-Mess* on the picture box with Ruff.

HOW COULD I BE SO WRONG!?!? I've been waiting impatiently for Critter-Mess Eve to arrive and for Saint Lick to…to…POOP ALL OVER THE CATCH-A-DOGGY-BONE KENNEL!!!

6 p.m.

It's no use, my person-pal. I got home hours ago and I've been trying to warn my family about the dreadful thing I found out, but they just don't understand Doglish.

It's useless! If I don't do something quick, my poor pet humans are going to wake up on Critter-Mess Day morning and find the whole kennel is piled high with stinky…PRESENTS!!

They'll never think I'm a GOOD BOY again if that happens. I'm going to have to take matters into my own paws. I've got just under a week until the big day and the POOPER FROM THE NORTH POLE arrives to do his worst.

THINK, JUNIOR, THINK!!

Monday

Check! Check! This is Secret Agent Junior, do you copy?

Right, my furless friend, I've been thinking and plotting lots of different ways to stop the dreaded Saint Lick from flying to our house and ruining Critter-Mess for us.

Lola's pet human has a bouncy tramp-o-line in her backyard, so at first I thought…

But I'd never get that thing up onto the roof.

Then I thought...

But I'd never find a bag big enough!

What am I going to do?!? If Mom-Lady and Jawjaw find out that I knew about this and didn't stop it, I'll be branded a BAD DOG for life.

Wednesday

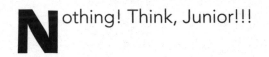

othing! Think, Junior!!!

Thursday

Still nothing…I wonder how long it would take to befriend the local RACCOONS, train them to eat intruders, then send them all up the chimney on Critter-Mess Eve to wait for our unwanted guest?

Hmmmm…probably too long…and I'm not sure they'd like it up there too much…

Friday

AAAAAAAAGH! I'm running out of time!!

Saturday

I never thought I'd say this, my furless friend, but I take it all back—the Howliday Season is a NIGHTMARE. It's terrible. Every time I close my eyes for a nap I have dreams of reindeer-pulled rascals doing their business in our lovely kennel. This is not the Critter-Mess-time I was hoping for!

Sunday

It gets worse! Tomorrow is Critter-Mess Eve and I've just found out that Grandmoo is coming to stay the night. She's going to sleep on the comfy squishy thing in the Picture Box Room. She'll be in prime position for POOP PERIL!!

CRITTER-MESS EVE

Okay, my furless friend, I've had an idea! Tonight is the night and there's no way I am just going to sit back and watch my poor, unsuspecting pet humans have their Howliday Season ruined.

I may not be able to stop Saint Lick from arriving in Hills Village, but I can certainly stop him from getting into the Catch-A-Doggy-Bone kennel. They don't call me the

INTERNATIONAL POOCH OF POWER for
nothing, you know!

INTERNATIONAL POOCH
OF POWER

Well, okay…no one calls me that, but they will when everybody realizes that I saved the happiest of howlidays.

Now it's just a waiting game…

12:23 p.m.

Grandmoo has just arrived with an armful of the most incredible-looking gifts, all wrapped with bows and sparkly paper. For the first time in days, I just got a tickle of excitement down my spine again. So long as I can keep the Dastardly Doo-Doo-er out, this could still be the BESTEST Critter-Mess ever.

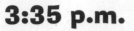

3:35 p.m.

The family has sat down to play some weird game with colored checkers going around a board. Ha! Just look at 'em. I don't think I've ever loved a bunch of humans more…even JAWJAW!

6 p.m.

Getting a little bored now…come on!!

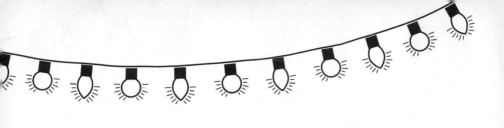

7 p.m.

This is TORTURE, my person-pal. I've been dreading tonight, but now I can't wait for everyone to go to bed so I can turn our kennel into a FLUSHING FORTRESS, too scary for any prowling pooper to venture inside.

8 p.m.

COME ON!!! I'M PRACTICALLY ITCHING TO GET GOING!!

Oh, hang on. That might just be fleas...

9 p.m.

It's finally time, my furless friend. Mom-Lady has ordered everybody off to their Sleep Rooms for an early night. All I have to do is curl up with Ruff, wait for him to fall asleep, and then sneak out for OPERATION POOP PATROL!!

11:38 p.m.

Shhhhhh! Don't make a sound or we'll wake everybody up. It's time, my person-pal...You stay here and I'll let you know when it's all over.

12:27 a.m.

Pssssst! Oh, sorry...did I wake you? It's done, my furless friend. The Catch-A-Doggy-Bone kennel is so filled with traps, there's no way Saint Lick will get away with his sticky plans. Uh-uh!

I found a load of the orange exploding vegetables from Fangsgiving (super squishy now) in the trash and put them all around Grandmoo. That'll protect her!

I put Jawjaw's building blocks along the
base of every door. Saint Lick will get a prickly
surprise if he steps on any of them.

I turned on the taps in the Rainy Poop Room and pulled the door shut. If he goes in there, he'll get washed halfway down the street. Ha ha!

There's a maze of toilet paper between the Critter-Mess tree and...well...just about everything. A tangle trap for sure!

Mom-Lady left a big bag
of little green sprouty
vegetables in the Food
Room. They made
excellent slippy-
sliders for all over
the floors.

That ought to do it, my person-pal. No
one comes into my kennel and leaves poopy
presents all over the place on my watch!

Now there's just a bit more waiting to be
done. Everyone will be so proud of me when
they see I've caught Saint Lick.

408

1 a.m.

Waiting…

1:23 a.m.

Waitin…

1:34 a.m.

Wai….

1:35 a.m.

zzzZZZZZZZZZZZ

CRITTER-MESS DAY!

7:12 a.m.

Aaaaaaagh! I must have fallen asleep. I've just woken up to the sound of yelling. It must be him! Saint Lick must have triggered one of my traps, my furless friend. Let's go see!!

8 a.m.

I DID IT, MY PERSON-PAL!

I ran out of Ruff's Sleep Room to find complete chaos! Grandmoo, Mom-Lady, Ruff, and Jawjaw were scrabbling around with water and exploded orange goop everywhere. Hundreds of green sprouty vegetables were bobbing about and the Critter-Mess tree was being washed down the hall in a cloud of soggy toilet paper.

I looked left and right, scanning the rooms for Saint Lick the Prowling Pooper, and you know what? He was nowhere to be seen!! I stopped that Dastardly Doo-Doo-er! Which means...

Well, whodathunk?! I never imagined when I started this second adventure in my Dog Diaries that I'd be saving Critter-Mess and making this the most memorable Howl-iday Season the Catch-A-Doggy-Bones had ever had.

My work is done here, my person-pal.

I don't think things could be any more fes-tively fantastic and I can't wait to go join my pack for a day of CRITTER-MESS CHEER!!

415

The Next Morning

Oh! Wait! One last thing, my furless friend.

Last night, after Mom-Lady had cleaned up all the mess left from my amazing Saint Lick traps (she was so impressed she wailed and screamed practically ALL DAY), Ruff and I went back to his Sleep Room and found something strange on his pillow.

417

Well, what do you know!? Saint Lick must have been so impressed by OPERATION POOP PATROL he left me my first-ever Critter-Mess gift. It's a black lumpy thing!! I'M A GOOD BOY FOR CERTAIN!!

How to speak Doglish

A human's essential guide to speaking paw-fect Doglish!

HOLIDAYS

Peoplish	Doglish
The Holiday Season	The Howliday Season
Thanksgiving	Fangsgiving
Christmas Day	Critter-Mess Day
New Year's Day	New Ears Day
Independence Day	Inky-pen-dance Day

PEOPLE

Peoplish	Doglish
Owner	Pet human
Grandma	Grandmoo
Grandpa	Grand-paw
Mom	Mom-lady
Georgia	Jawjaw
Rafe	Ruff
Khatchadorian	Catch-A-Doggy-Bone
Santa Claus	Saint Lick

PLACES

Peoplish	Doglish
House	Kennel
Bedroom	Sleep Room
Kitchen	Food Room
Bathroom	Rainy Poop Room
Livingroom	Picture Box Room

THINGS

Peoplish	Doglish
Fridge	Coldy frosty tall thing
Oven	Hot fire box
TV	Picture box
Sofa	Comfy squishy thing
Car	Moving people-box on wheels
Telephone	Chatty-ear-stick
Mobile phone	Talky box
Icicles	Ace-icles

Read on for some fun activities!

You Will Need...

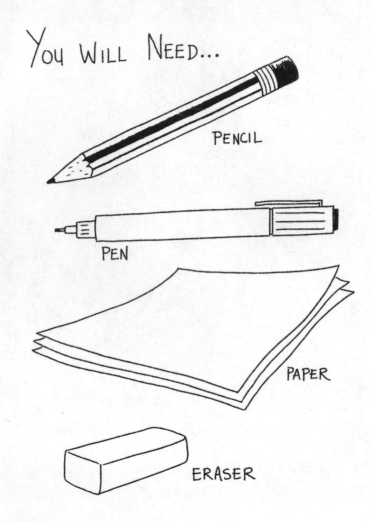

PENCIL

PEN

PAPER

ERASER

★ IN PENCIL,
   DRAW 3 CIRCLES
   LIKE THIS...

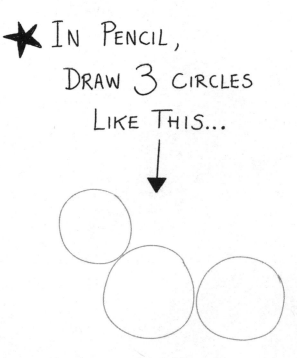

★ DRAW LINES TO CONNECT THE 3 CIRCLES...

★ ADD A SNOUT TO THIS CIRCLE

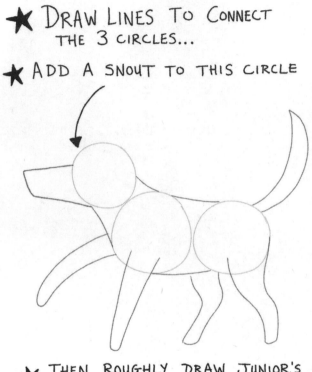

★ THEN ROUGHLY DRAW JUNIOR'S LEGS AND TAIL...

★ Now Using The Pen, Draw A JAGGED LINE AROUND THE SHAPES TO GIVE JUNIOR A FURRY OUTLINE.

★ ADD IN A MOUTH HERE...

★ AND A COLLAR.

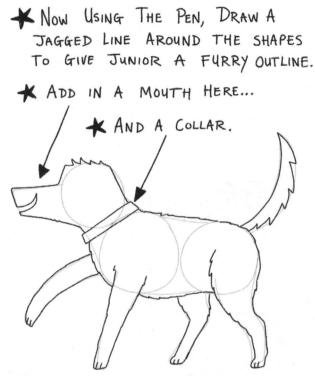

★ THEN ERASE YOUR PENCIL LINES...

★ DRAW 2 SMALL CIRCLES FOR
JUNIOR'S EYES.

★ THEN ADD EARS AND A NOSE...

⭐ FINALLY...

ADD DOTS TO THE EYES,
DRAW EYEBROWS
THEN COLOR JUNIOR'S NOSE
AND EARS IN BLACK...

NOW STAND BACK AND ADMIRE YOUR WORK!

ODIN ONE OUT!

One of the Odins below looks different to the others!
Which one is the odd one out?

1

2

3

4

5

6

7

8

9

HOW MANY CAN YOU SPOT?

About the Authors

JAMES PAT-MY-HEAD-ERSON is the international bestselling author of the poochilicious Middle School, I Funny, Jacky Ha-Ha, Treasure Hunters, and House of Robots series, as well as *Word of Mouse, Max Einstein: The Genius Experiment, Pottymouth and Stoopid,* and *Laugh Out Loud.* James Patterson's books have sold more than 400 million copies kennel-wide, making him one of the biggest-selling GOOD BOYS of all time. He lives in Florida.

Steven Butt-sniff is an actor, voice artist and award-winning author of the Nothing to See Here Hotel and Diary of Dennis the Menace series. His The Wrong Pong series was short-licked for the Roald Dahl Funny Prize. He is also the host of World Bark Day's The Biggest Book Show on Earth.

Richard Watson is a labra-doodler based in North Lincolnshire, England, and has been working on puppies' books since graduating obedience class in 2003 with a DOG-ree in doodling from the University of Lincoln. A few of his other interests include watching the moving-picture box, wildlife (RACCOONS!), and music.

Don't miss Junior's latest adventure in

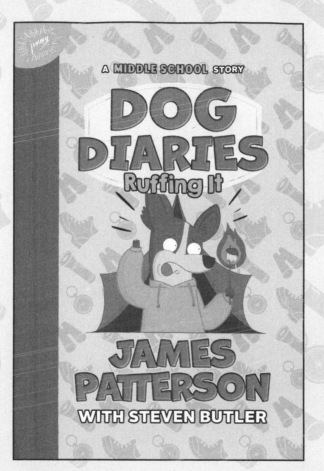

APRIL 19, 2021

I have one word for you, my person-pal...WE'RE GOING ON VACATION!

Okay...okay...that was four words, I know, but I'm just a little over-excited right now and can't help it! My ears are twitchy, my jowls are drooly, and I'm giving serious thought to spending the entire afternoon having one long HIP-HOORAY-HOUNDY-HOWL!

Let me explain…right now, my amazing furless person-pack of humans, THE CATCH-A-DOGGY-BONE PACK, and I are about to clamber into the moving people-box on wheels and head out of Hills Village, hitting the road for a really real surprise adventure!

I wonder what it'll be! Where in the world is Mom-Lady taking us? AGH! I'M SO EXCITED! I've been waiting for the chance to go on the vacation of a lifetime for…well…A LIFE-TIME! HAHA!

My best buddy, Ruff, and I are bound to have the most amazing time, I just know it, and the thought of vacationing with him has made my tail waggier than EVER! I have the most terrific pet human in all of Hills Village, make no mistake. No, scratch that…the world! No, scratch that…THE UNIVERSE!

Ruff makes me want to yip-yap with joy and

do a happy dance from daybreak to snooze time, and now…we're finally getting the chance to snuffle off into the sunset together for a whole week of playing ball, nose-boops, snacking, and snoozing! It's going to be bliss.

Well…umm…I'm sure it is. Mom-Lady has been super-secretive about where we're actually heading, but I can tell she's giddy as a greyhound who just stole Grandmoo's slipper, so it has to be great!

But I'm getting ahead of myself…

Introductions are extremely important to us pooches. And I'd say it's time for ours.

If we've already met and you've read my AMAZING Dog Diaries before…Welcome back, my person-pal! I'm so happy you decided to come along for another spot of masterful mischief!

If you've never pawed through any of my mutt manuals before, however, I should probably start by telling you that I'm Junior... Junior Catch-A-Doggy-Bone... HELLO! It's a pleasure to sniff you!

I should also try to shed a little light on some of the BARKTASTIC and FUR-RAISING things that have happened to me since I came to live in the Catch-A-Doggy-Bone kennel, or you'll have no idea what I'm barking on about.

Y'see, I've had my fair share of crazy scrapes with obedience classes, canine criminals, midnight feasts, stolen treasured trinkets, junkyard hijinks, terrifying turkeys, dandy dog shows, howly wieners, vicious vacuum cleaners, and bowlfuls of Meaty-Giblet-Jumble-Chum. But, one of the most spine-jangling, MOST HOUNDY HEART-POUNDING moments of all, was the time I thought we were going on vacation to HOLLYWOOD! Sounds terrific, right? WRONG!

I tell you, my person-pal, I couldn't have been more excited to bark my way along the boulevards of TinkleTown (I think that's what they call it) and snuffle through those streets paved with sausage meat. So, you can imagine how horrified I was when it all went totally bonkers, and my pooch-pack and I ended up in a hotel for...for...this isn't easy to say. We ended up in a hotel for...VEGETARIAN DOGS!

OH, THE TERROR!

I don't want to ruin that story for you in case you haven't read it, and I certainly don't want to spend even one more second thinking about that VEG-O-RIFIC disaster. Ugh! It makes me shudder just thinking about it.

It goes without saying that this mangy
mutt is definitely in need of his first ever

dream vacation without any of the vexation.
Haha!

Yep! A little me-time to stretch my paws
and feel the wind in my tail is just what the
veterinarian ordered...and now it's finally
happening!

It started two days ago. C'mon...I'll tell you
all about it.